W9-CJE-525

SHOTGUN GUARD

SHOTGUN GUARD

D. B. NEWTON

THORNDIKE
CHIVERS

This Large Print edition is published by Thorndike Press, Waterville, Maine, USA and by BBC Audiobooks Ltd, Bath, England.

Thorndike Press, a part of Gale, Cengage Learning.

Set in 16 pt. Plantin.

LIBRARY OF CONGRESS CATALOGING-IN-PUBLICATION DATA

Bennett, Dwight, 1916–
  Shotgun guard / by D.B. Newton. — Large print ed.
    p. cm. — (Thorndike Press large print western)
  Originally published: Bath : Gunsmoke, 1950.
  ISBN-13: 978-1-4104-2961-2
  ISBN-10: 1-4104-2961-X
  1. Large type books. I. Title.
PS3527.E9178S56 2010
813'.52—dc22   2010020050

BRITISH LIBRARY CATALOGUING-IN-PUBLICATION DATA AVAILABLE

Published in 2010 in the U.S. by arrangement with Golden West Literary Agency.

Published in 2011 in the U.K. by arrangement with Golden West Literary Agency.

U.K. Hardcover: 978 1 408 49283 3 (Chivers Large Print)
U.K. Softcover: 978 1 408 49284 0 (Camden Large Print)

Printed in the United States of America
1 2 3 4 5 6 7 14 13 12 11 10

SHOTGUN GUARD

CHAPTER ONE

Because the twice-weekly feeder stage bound for the mining regions west of Dragoon was scheduled to roll at daybreak, Dan Temple had had to knock off early, as usual, and clean up for his ten-mile ride to town. As usual he left a thousand. chores unfinished — it was no cinch, building a homestead ranch in the one day out of three that could be spared from his regular job of riding shotgun for the Great Western line. Forking a clean-limbed chestnut gelding, he came into Dragoon now as the last colors of sunset were laying golden fire across the western rims. And discouragement, and a bone-deep tiredness, rode with him.

The golden magic of the hour could turn this drab place almost beautiful; but by the time Temple had his horse settled in its customary stall at the livery barn, the glow had got out of things and dusk, like a gray smoke, was pouring across the flatlands. He made his way without haste along a cinder path flanked by gaunt and dusty cottonwoods, heading for the blocky shape of the hotel. A meal, and then bed: such was the only program he contemplated, in view of the hour at which he'd have to rise next morning.

Dusk softened the weary harshness of a face that was dark from sun and wind, perhaps a little gaunted, with a small white scar marring the high bridge of the nose. Dark hair, worn long, had already begun to gray a little at the temples — not from years, for this man was still young, only a bit over thirty. But he was a man carrying the burden of two full-time jobs, pouring out too much of his strength upon them. Lately, he was beginning to suspect that he had picked a poor time of life for new beginnings, for setting a fresh course after the random years of a youth not wisely spent. . . .

The lamps of the hotel dining room were already lighted; night stained the windows a rich, deep hue. About half the tables were occupied. As Temple halted briefly in the fringed doorway leading off the lobby, a youngish chap eating alone glanced up and nodded curt greeting. Temple returned the nod and moved forward, threading his way among the other tables, until he reached the one at which Abel Ramsey was seated.

"Evening," he said.

With his mouth full, Ramsey indicated the chair opposite him and Dan Temple slacked into it, gunharness creaking. He dropped his hat to the floor beside him and settled back tiredly, crossing his legs beneath the table and waiting for his boss to speak.

A thin, tight-strung man, this Ramsey, with sallow skin and knobby wrists and spiky, lifeless brown hair; he looked rather like one who had grown too fast as a boy and never had time since to fill out to maturity. He took a swallow of coffee now, set the cup down and glanced across at Dan while he toyed nervously with the handle of it.

"You set for tomorrow morning?"

"Certainly," said Temple, and shrugged a little. "What's so special about tomorrow? Nothing more than the ordinary payroll run to Antelope, is it?"

"I suppose not," muttered Ramsey, without conviction. He was always like this, Dan observed. You could almost tell, from his varying degree of nervousness, the strong-box contents of any given shipment before ever it hit the stage road.

"You worry too much," said Dan. "You

act as though we lost a shipment every other week, whereas up to now we've kept a perfect record. Why can't you relax? It's my job to see the payrolls get through!"

The other stabbed him a look. "Yes," he said. "That's all it is to you — a job that's finished when you step down off the box at the end of a run. This thing isn't saddled on your shoulders permanently — day and night."

"That," said Dan, coolly, "I count as my reward for not being the son of old Saul Ramsey. But even he wouldn't have lived long enough to build a staging business, if he'd stayed awake nights worrying about every coach and wagon he had out on the roads!"

"All right!" snapped young Ramsey, his eyes dangerous. "Suppose we drop the subject?"

Dan Temple shrugged again and turned to consider his order, as a thick-limbed waitress came to set out water glass and cutlery in front of him.

There was heavy silence between the two of them, after that, during all the time it took Ramsey to finish his meal. He rose finally, shoved a niggardly tip beneath his plate and took a soft, narrow-brimmed hat from a hook in the wall. For a moment he hesitated, looking down at Temple as though he would have liked to add something further; but in the end he turned away from Dan's cool regard and strode off, to vanish through the lobby entrance.

Dan Temple watched him go, thinking that an odd relationship existed between him and his employer — this weakling son of a hard-fisted stage line builder, whose father's death six months ago had thrown onto his incompetent shoulders the management of Great Western Express. . . .

His own meal finished, Dan paid and went out for a turn along the cinder walk before the hotel, to enjoy a smoke and take in a little of the crispness of the spring evening before climbing to the room he reserved here for his nights in Dragoon town. There was still a band of lemon-yellow light in the sky, above the sharp-etched outlines of the western hills. Venus shone there, a bright pinprick of silver. A chill that had teeth in it flowed across the dark plain, where amid sage and rolling bunch grass the town spread its crisscross of streets and its studding of lampglow.

A ranch wagon came toward him along the street, laying a thin film and tang of dust into the coolness. Dan Temple stood and watched it, idly, thinking he knew the rig but not really certain until a voice suddenly spoke his name. The horses veered, pulled over toward the place where he stood revealed in a spilling of light from an unshaded window behind him. The team halted and Dan touched hatbrim as he greeted the small figure that held the reins. "Well, Ruth!" he said; and, nodding to the taller of the pair on the high seat, "How are you, Tom?"

The man returned the nod curtly, the shape and voice of him faintly disapproving as he answered, "I'll do, I reckon." But there was warmth in the girl, and a real friendliness. She began talking at once, her words overlaying Tom McNeil's chill greeting.

"I just came from Rafferty's, before he closed up a few minutes ago," she told the man in the path. "He had an order of yours — a couple of spools of wire he said you'd been looking for, and it just came in today."

"Well, that's good news," said Temple. "I've been digging out that spring and I want to get a fence to keep the cattle away. I'll have to see about hauling it out to the place soon as I get back from the run tomorrow."

"It's already taken care of," she told him quickly, and jerked her head toward the wagonbox behind her. "I figured you'd be wanting the wire so I had Rafferty dump it in with our stuff. We can drop it off on our way home to the Cross C."

Dan Temple frowned. "But that isn't on your way, Ruth. It's a good five miles out of it. Mighty neighborly of you, but I don't like you bothering."

She replied in a voice that was subtly altered, almost abrupt. "No bother. What's a neighbor for?"

"Not for doing a man's chores for him, certainly. Really, you've done so much already I don't know how I can repay you. It worries me."

"Don't let it."

He couldn't fail to sense the quick change in her; the warmth had gone and a cool distance seemed to have drawn between them. It was like this, always, with her, and these alterations in her manner were a constant source of puzzlement to Dan Temple. Now, as he fumbled for the words to answer her, gaunt Tom McNeil shifted on the wagonseat and mumbled, "If you're set on ridin' out of our way we better get started. It's a far piece."

The girl nodded agreement, and lifted the reins in firm, strong hands. She looked at Dan, again, for the brief space of a breath, and then gave him a careless "Goodnight!"

13

A moment later the leathers snapped and stung at the rumps of the horses and Temple stood watching the rig draw away from him into the darkness.

He took a deep drag at his cigarette, dropped it into the cinders and set a boot on it. Now, what had he said? As so often after one of these inconclusive scenes with the Chess girl, he found himself rehearsing them line by line and searching out, without success, the causes of her abrupt changes of mood. Tom McNeil, of course, disliked him heartily, with a certain stubborn intolerance; but at least he was honest about it and, with it all, as civil as custom demanded. Dan Temple could hardly mind that. But though he liked Ruth Chess, he did mind and rather resent a changeableness that had no explanation. . . .

He shrugged, putting the thing out of his mind as he heeled about and turned back to the hotel. The saffron light had gone from the west now. Night was complete, and it carried the sharp edge of a winter only just spent. Temple crossed the deep veranda, got his key from the board behind the lobby desk and climbed the stairway to his room off the second floor corridor.

He knew this room well; he needed no lamp to find his way around in it and now he undressed in the dark, hanging his clothing on the single chair, setting his boots beneath the edge of the bed. He ran the window open, stood a moment to let a mounting night wind blow about his naked body.

Afterwards, early as it was, Dan Temple pulled down the covers of the swaybacked bed and stretched himself upon its hard and unyielding mattress. In a matter of minutes he was asleep.

He could have been like that for only a little while when a hard-knuckled pounding on the door brought him suddenly awake and he lay scowling, regathering his senses. He could make out the shadow of a pair of boots, breaking the pencil line of light across the bottom of the door. The bed creaked faintly under him, as he stirred reluctantly.

"What is it?"

His only answer was more of the heavy, insistent knocking, and throwing back the covers he called sharply, "Well, just a minute, will you?" Reaching his jeans off the chair he dragged them on and groped his way to the table where he found a lamp and got it burning. He had had just enough sleep to blur his reflexes and make his eyes sting to the stab of the lamplight, and this had him scowling as he padded to the door, barefooted and naked to the waist, and jerked it open.

The man in the doorway was not one he had seen before. He was a big fellow, as tall as Dan and solidly built. He was blond, with crisp light hair, good-looking features, a smile that showed square, white teeth. In a tweed coat and riding breeches and knee-high boots, he seemed to fill the entrance with a brash, aggressive virility.

His voice was deep and boomed out of him even when he tried to hold it down. "You're this Dan Temple, are you?"

Still irritable from awakening, the other said shortly, "That's my name."

"Lawler is mine. Reed Lawler. Sorry for breaking in on you like this; I got your room number downstairs and the clerk said you'd be pulling out early in the morning, and I wanted to talk to you. I'll try not to take much of your time."

Temple shrugged. "Come in then."

His visitor entered. Temple cleared the rest of his clothing off the room's only chair, and turned to the window to close it and shut the night wind out. He looked at his visitor. "Well?"

Lawler had taken the chair; he crossed his legs, tilted back with his hat on one knee and his thumbs hooked into the waistband

16

of expensive tweeds. Lamplight glinted in the crisp yellow of his short-cropped hair as he nodded.

"I've got a proposition for you, Temple. I've done some talking around, the few days I've been in this country; I've heard about what you're doing, out on that homestead section. Didn't seem at first you could be the same Dan Temple I was thinking of, but I guess you are, at that. And with your reputation and your talent, I figure you're the man I want."

Dan Temple folded his arms and leaned his naked back against the wall, beside the window. He looked at the other without thawing. "The only talent I've got is one for using a sixgun. The reputation is the kind that goes with it. I'm not too proud of either; and I don't think I'd care for your — proposition."

The man's teeth flashed in a brazen smile. "Don't jump to conclusions. Nothing crooked about this — I know you'd never hire out your gun, except legitimately. Right now, I believe, you're riding shotgun for the Ramseys. I'm ready to up by a half whatever they're paying you, to do the same work for me."

"You still don't understand. I'm a rancher now — or trying to be, on what I earn shotgunning. My roots are set; I couldn't leave this range just for an offer of good pay."

"Who mentioned leaving?" murmured Lawler. "I'm starting a new stage and freight business — right here, out of Dragoon. And in competition with the Ramseys!"

For a long moment Dan Temple could only stare at him. "But — there isn't enough business for two lines. Great Western gives good enough service to hold what there is."

"I didn't ask your advice!" said Lawler, coldly. "I know what I'm doing — and I got money to back me. Meanwhile, there's this job if you want it. The pay starts immediately — and until I'm ready to start rolling, you can go back to that homestead ranch and get caught up on your work there; it might even be a matter of weeks yet. Anything wrong with that offer?"

"Yes!" snapped Temple, suddenly angry. "The smell! What you're really asking me to do is sell out the Ramseys — leave them stuck without a shotgun guard, and on no notice whatever!"

A brief, hard silence fell upon the end of that speech. But then Reed Lawler's smile returned, confident and mocking.

"As far as that's concerned," he pointed out, "Great Western has been going downhill, steadily, ever since the old man died. Those two spoiled brats of his can't last much longer — they haven't the brains or instinct for this business. Seems to me, friend, it's better to make it short, and merciful. Better to break them — like this!" He snapped his fingers, the sound sharp in the stillness.

Dan Temple had shoved away from the wall. He came toward Lawler a step or two. The wash of light from the lamp, that showed the dinginess of the room — the yellowed wallpaper, the frayed carpet worn through to the boards in front of the washstand, the tarnished brass of the rumpled bed — showed also the tense movement of a muscle in the flat plane of his cheek.

He said, quietly, "I'd advise you to get out of here!"

"Oh!" The other only looked at him. "I came to you first, Temple — and certainly not because I pegged you for a fool! News of what I'm planning will be all over town, in a day or two. I think then you'll see the light — when that spineless Abel Ramsey starts squirming."

"Get out!"

"All right." The blond man came easily to his feet, facing Temple with that same mocking look. "Maybe," he suggested softly, "I oughtn't to forget there's a woman in this — a damnably handsome woman. I've seen this Stella Ramsey. Twice as much spunk to her as that weak-kneed brother. In your boots, maybe I wouldn't be in too big a hurry, either, to pass up a chance at —"

Temple hit him, without warning, driving the unfinished speech back into the toothy smile. There was a savage anger in his blow and it sent Lawler's head snapping back upon the solid, pillar-like neck. With a grunt of pain he whirled half around; the chair behind him got in the way and he went crashing down, his weight splintering one of its legs with a crack that echoed the meaty slap of fist against flesh.

Dan Temple looked at the man he had felled, with a kind of slow astonishment building in him. The thing had been done in a blind and unpremeditated spurt of rage. Now he watched Reed Lawler roll clear of the wreckage and come to his knees, and saw the imprint of fury on him.

Lawler's face had lost much of its sleek good looks. There was angry color in the broad features, a black ugliness that drew his lips away from hard-clamped teeth. A trickle of blood began and crept slowly down at the corner of his mouth. And, kneeling like that, he started to lift right

20

hand toward his armpit, where the sag of the tweed coat fell away and revealed what was strapped snugly in place there.

But Lawler did not touch the gun. Instead, dropping his hand reluctantly, he looked away from Dan and spotted his soft-brimmed hat where it had fallen. He picked it up, and came slowly to his feet, darkness shielding his real emotion in his eyes.

He said, "You hit hard, friend. . . ."

Turning, suddenly, he wrenched open the door, strode through and was gone down the narrow hallway, leaving the door open behind him. A frown rode Temple's dark face as he stepped to the door and closed it, and stood for a long moment with his hand upon the knob.

He didn't like any part of this, of what had been done and said. . . .

CHAPTER TWO

Sunlight was kind to Stella Ramsey. It revealed the perfection of a flawless, milk-white skin; more than that, its probing fingers were always discovering rich and unexpected glints of golden flame within the coppery beauty of her hair. Stella was not at all unaware of this. She had formed the instinctive habit of toying with her heavy auburn tresses, of running a hand up under them while she tossed her head a little to shake them out and let them fall again. It was a pretty gesture, artful and at the same time charming.

So, at least, Dan Temple thought it as he came into the stage line office and saw her at her desk by the window, one arm raised in that way she had, so that, perhaps unconsciously, her breasts were lifted and the stuff of her dress drawn tight across them. The dress was green, almost matching the color of her eyes. She looked up as the door closed and gave Dan a slow, cool smile.

"Good morning, Dan."

They were not alone; a couple of drummers and a stock buyer were loitering on the bench by the door, waiting for the stage to make up, their luggage at their feet and their interest more or less openly centered on the young woman at the desk. Dan Temple nodded to them briefly, and dropping his leather jacket across the railing that divided the big room, pushed through the swinging gate.

He was still in not too good a mood. He spoke to the girl, went to a rack fastened to the rear wall of the office that held a brace of double-barreled shotguns. He chose one, looked briefly to its mechanism and the

22

shining, carefully oiled tubes. Then, taking a box of shells from the top of the cabinet he loaded both chambers of the shotgun, dropped the rest of the box into a pocket.

The girl had risen from her desk and walked casually over to watch him work. Dan looked at her now, and he shoved the hat back on his head. "Your brother around this morning?"

"Down at the stable, seeing to the hitching-up. Becker has gone with Mr. Evans to the bank to get the payroll. I've got them on schedule this morning, Dan. You'll be rolling out of here on the nose!"

Her pride in this was evident — her asking for his approval. She wanted him to see that by bringing her force to bear on the vacillating and unsure brother who was now the nominal manager of Great Western, it could be run almost as efficiently and profitably as under the firm hand of their late father. He nodded, admiration open in his glance as he looked at this tall, cooly beautiful and self-assured young woman.

He said, "That's all you need to do — get this service back on schedule and then keep it there. Otherwise," he added, sobering, "you might have a fight on your hands."

A frown touched her clear brow. "What do you mean?"

Dan told her, then, about his visitor of the night before. As he talked he saw a look that was new to him come into Stella Ramsey's face — defiant, angrily determined. "So this Lawler wants to break Great Western!" she cried. "Well, let him try! We'll give him a fight; it might be the very thing we need to put a little backbone into Abel. And with you on our side, Dan — he'll have a tough time beating us."

She placed a slim hand upon his arm and let it rest there — an intimate gesture, that brought its quick response. But just then the morning stage came rolling up from the direction of the stable yard, and Dan Temple turned away, carrying the shotgun and taking his leather coat from the railing as he pushed through the swinging gate.

The passengers were already filing outside the office, to await with carpetbags and drummers' sample cases their chance to load into the big coach. Morning sun, slanting into the street, touched gold from the dust the restless six-horse team stirred up to send drifting before an early breeze. Dan stepped around to the front wheel, and tossed his jacket up to be caught by the driver — a gaunt, surly-visaged man named Pearson.

He did not swing up to the box himself,

just yet, but stayed where he was, to roll a smoke and enjoy the few minutes remaining before he must resign himself to the jolt and jar of the lumbering stage.

Downstreet, two men came along the cinder path from the direction of the bank, carrying between them the small, stout express box which constituted Dan's particular charge and responsibility — the biweekly payroll shipment for the syndicate-owned Yellow Jack mine, up in the timbered hills. The shorter of the two was John Evans, the syndicate's local manager, a fussy individual, of a soft paunchiness born of good food and sedentary living. He was a competent enough executive, Dan Temple supposed — at least, he kept his job and seemed to please his Eastern bosses. But he wasn't one you'd be apt to notice very much, one way or another.

Dan nodded a curt greeting and looked at the second man. "All right, Becker. Give me a hand up with it — and try not to drop it this time."

Paul Becker was the Ramsey's chief clerk, another Easterner — a cold, unfriendly man who had never in six months' time lowered the icy wall of half-suspicious reserve or spoken more than a dozen words to Dan. He owned none of Temple's hardness of body and Dan all but took the express box away from him, hoisting it up the side of the coach.

"Now, the gun," he ordered, when the box had been stowed in place beneath the seat. Paul Becker got the weapon from where Dan had left it leaning against the wheel, and handed it up to him sullenly. There seemed to be a very definite, though unexplained, hostility between these two.

By now the coach was loaded; Sim Pearson had finished stowing luggage into the rear boot and had its leather cover strapped down, and he climbed again to his place, stuffing the waybill Stella Ramsey had given him into a pocket of his woolen shirt. Dan Temple settled back upon the hard seat beside him in resignation to the long and weary miles to come, as Pearson lifted his whip out of the socket.

Suddenly, to the riflelike crack of buckskin poppers and a shattering whoop that broke from Sim's deep lungs, the horses surged into the collars. The heavy stage rolled forward, with a jolt that must have jarred the passengers below if they weren't prepared for it.

Looking back, Dan had a last glimpse of Stella Ramsey in the office doorway — a tall, slim shape in green, one hand lifted

26

under the thick fall of heavy copper curls; she tossed her head, and slanting sunlight gleamed briefly in the beauty of her hair as it swept about her shoulders. Then she was lost in a swirl of filming dust and they rolled on down the wide main street, recklessly gathering speed.

Passers-by whooped from the edge of the dust strip; a rider on a cowpony pulled aside hastily and cursed good-naturedly. And, as they pounded past the hotel, Dan sighted the blocky figure of the man who stood at the top of the broad steps, one forearm slanted against a roof support, the other hand raised to his lips holding a cigar. Reed Lawler. . . . His blond head swiveled on solid shoulders as he watched the coach rock by.

Afterwards, the last scattered buildings of Dragoon town flashed away and the open road twisted ahead across tawny, rolling stretches of bunch grass and sage toward the lifting timber hills. Dan Temple shifted into a more comfortable position, his shotgun between his knees, gray eyes squinted against the slip of wind and the smoke of his own cigarette battering back against his face.

They were not beauties, these Great Western stages. Sun-scorch and scouring sand and snow had long ago wiped them clean of paint and dug deep gouges in the paneling, and the leather of the seats was lumpy and indented to the fit of countless travelers. But they had been built to last, and to withstand the worst dangers of the run up across the hills and twisting mountain roads to the mining camps and, on over the hump, to the stock ranges beyond.

Moreover, they were in the finest of running condition. That had been a religion with old Saul Ramsey and one he had ingrained in his barnmen and maintenance crews; it was something even the lax administration of his son had not affected. Nearly silent except for the clucking of the axles in the sandboxes, the big coach rolled on through the morning, now, rocking on its thoroughbraces with every dip and swell of the rutted road.

An hour passed. The horses were into the collars, climbing. They had left the flat rangeland; spurs of timber lifted about them, naked granite upthrusts interspersing scattered spruce and juniper. Now brown snow-water ran rushing along a canyon bottom, footing a steep drop just below the big offside wheels. Temple dozed a little, nodding, beside the surly, lantern-jawed Pearson.

The road topped out onto a narrow benchland, with the higher hills ahead. The sun drew a pungent fragrance from thick-growing, stunted cedar that crowded the trace, here. Dust whispered beneath the wheels, muffling the hoofbeats of the horses and lifting to hang in a fog and settle again, yellowly. Then they were climbing once more, and heavier timber began closing in — tall yellow pines, thick-boled, that seemed to scrape the sky as they wheeled away overhead.

Sim Pearson knew just how much he could demand of his horses. Precisely when their lagging gait threatened to break stride, he hauled them in for the first breather at a place where, just beyond, the way pointed steeply upward through a narrow, granite-walled gap.

Kicking on the brake, he leaned far over and yelled sourly down to his passengers: "Stretch your legs here, if you've a mind to." Groans and curses greeted his suggestion; as the big coach rocked to a halt on its leather thoroughbraces, the doors were pushed open and the trio within crawled forth for a few welcome minutes on solid ground.

Dan Temple, stretching, laid the shotgun aside and threw a booted leg across preparatory to climbing down. He was in that awkward position when he saw the pair of masked men walking out of the trees hard beside the road. He halted that way, staring.

The two were oddly matched, one being tall and spare of shape and the other much shorter, with a breadth of body that was almost distorted and hinted of great muscular strength. They were indiscriminately garbed in worn range clothing, but the gunbelts and holsters strapped to them looked well-cared-for. The shorter of the pair had a sixgun leveled in his massive fist. The other carried an oil-stocked Winchester saddle gun cradled against his thin waist, its muzzle tilted and trained squarely on Temple.

From under the blue neck cloth that covered all his face below the eyes he said sharply, "Hold it right there, Buster! And anyone else that moves is asking for a bullet!"

A startled squawk broke from one of the passengers, but that was all. No one offered any resistance in the face of those drawn guns. At an order from the second bandit, the three passengers quickly lined up beside the coach, arms lifted. He stepped close and fanned them for weapons but found only one of them armed. That was the stock buyer, who had a hand gun in a pocket of his coat. The thick-bodied man captured this and tossed it from him into the undergrowth, the high sun making a smear of reflected light as the gun went end for end and thudded dully out of sight. He stepped back then, satisfied, and said in a guttural voice, "They're clean!"

The taller man had not taken his attention for an instant from the two on the driver's seat. Pearson had been caught there, under the muzzle of the rifle with which he also pinned Dan Temple in his place. The driver was obviously unarmed; now the man with the Winchester ordered sharply, "All right — the yahoo! Reach over with your left hand — the *left* one, mind you — and take the gun out of the other fellow's holster and let's have it down here at my feet. But careful — you understand?"

Sim Pearson had no choice. His face crimson with choking rage, he followed instructions; he took the sixgun gingerly and, leaning across Temple, chucked it over. It threw up a quick puff of gritty dust as it landed. Then, waved back by a gesture of the rifle barrel, he withdrew to his own end of the seat — crouched and tense, a figure of angry indignation.

As for Dan Temple, he had not moved at all from the first moment the pair with the guns showed at the edge of the trees hard by. A quick, tingling tightness was in his body, sharpness in his gray stare; but nothing of this showed. Unspeaking, he looked down at the masked face, at expressionless agate eyes that held no depths to them. He did not fail to notice when a quick breath of wind caught the edge of the blue cloth, flipped it briefly aside to reveal, though for an instant only, a glimpse of dark spade beard cut square below the narrow, pointed jaw.

The man said, "Throw down the box."

Dan made no move. "You're making a mistake," he said. "I think you'd better not go ahead with this."

The eyes, the voice, held no change. "I said throw it down!"

For just an instant a challenge lay between the two of them, a wordless interchange that no other man there could sense or read. Then Dan Temple moved. He moved forward, reaching into the boot.

The shiny twin tubes of the shotgun lay there, and he heard Pearson's sharp intake of breath as the driver thought he saw his intent. But Dan made no play to grab the shotgun. Instead, he seized the heavy express box and, straightening, set it on the edge of the boot and shoved it over. It struck the ground on an edge, went on over to a side. The tall man nodded, and then threw a quick order to his companion: "Get it, and make for the horses. I'll follow you!"

The box was all they wanted, apparently; there had been no play to rob the passengers of such valuables as might be found on them. The second man quickly sheathed his gun and, bending over the box, came up with it in his big hands as easily as though it held no weight whatsoever. An instant later he was hurrying off with it into the trees, toward where the pair obviously had horses waiting. The taller man retreated more slowly, moving backward, his rifle still leveled.

At Dan's side, Sim Pearson's breathing sounded hoarsely. Dan knew what he was thinking — knew he was wondering about that shotgun, and why the other man hadn't attempted to use it. Sim would have made a try, regardless of danger and the small protection that stage boot would have been from steel-jacketed, high-powered rifle shells at close range. Sim was that kind of a reckless fool.

And now, in fact, Sim did try it. The tall man had almost reached the shadowy wall of the pines when with a grunt of expelled breath Pearson flung himself to his knees, gloved hands seizing the shotgun and coming up with it. A strange accident happened, then. Just as the twin muzzles cleared the side of the boot and swung into line on the escaping bandit, it connected with Dan Temple's elbow and somehow, was deflected sharply upward. The twin triggers jerked under Pearson's hand and both barrels went off, discharging in a great roar of sound and crashing hail of deadly shot that were directed toward the blue sky and the gun-gilded pine tops. The horses, frightened, jumped and the coach rocked against the set brake.

Then the echoes of the explosion died. The bandits were gone, unscathed. In the sudden, startling stillness, the sound of a pair of quickly galloping horses took form somewhere beyond the trees and as quickly faded out.

Dan Temple looked at Pearson, left with the empty shotgun still smoking in his hands, and he saw the face of the man growing redder as crimson blood suffused it. Words struggled on Pearson's tongue, unable to find expression. Dan said quietly, "Sorry! You might have got him if my elbow hadn't interfered. It was a try, anyhow."

He turned, then, and went down the side of the coach.

34

An excited babble had started among the passengers as they realized the moment of danger was over for them; this was an event they would all be talking about for a good many days to come. Dan shrugged away the questions they hurled at him: "How much was in the box, mister?" "Think there's any chance of getting it back?" "Who fired the shot?" He leaned, picked his gun from the dust and blew the grit out of it, spinning the cylinder. This reminded the stock buyer of the weapon that had been taken from his own pocket and he went burrowing for it in the undergrowth beside the road, coming up with it after a moment of searching.

Then Sim Pearson's harsh command came down from the driver's seat. "Get in! All of you — and make it quick!"

The passengers scrambled aboard, and Dan resumed his own place. He had hardly settled onto the cushion when Pearson had the brake kicked off and was yelling at the horses. In some surprise, Dan realized the man was turning the stage.

A passenger thrust his head out of the window. "Hey! What's happening? We want to go on to Antelope!"

"You can wait a while!" Pearson yelled back at him. "Because this stage is heading back to Dragoon! The schedule is all shot to hell anyway — and the quicker the sheriff knows about this, the more chance of stopping those crooks before they get clean away into the hills with their loot."

All three of the men below were hanging out the windows now, protesting heatedly. But Sim Pearson was not one to be dissuaded once his mind was set. Dan Temple knew this; he looked at the other's grim, red-hued face, saw the hard determination in it. He read something else, too, and didn't like what it promised. This thought put foreboding in him, as he clung to the swaying seat and watched Sim Pearson lash his horses into a frantic run, back down the miles toward Dragoon.

CHAPTER THREE

Sheriff Tyler Gentry was a big man, square and blocky of figure, with iron-gray hair and a face that had something of the quality of iron about it, too. Only the eyes seemed alive in it, or possessed of any human quality; but they were amazingly expressive eyes, that could warm to friendship or harden with dislike, while the thin-lipped mouth and hard jaw remained clamped in the unyielding expression of the professional manhunter.

His implacable features showed nothing at all as he came bruskly into the Great Western's office, shouldering through the excited crowd that had gathered around the stage coach outside. It was an incident without parallel for the stage to return to home station this way, its run interrupted, and come funneling red dust along the town's streets in a dead run for the office, the horses lathered and near spent. Half the town seemed to have congested about it, within a matter of minutes, but so far their curiosity had received no satisfaction; because neither the driver nor the guard were offering any information, and the passengers, who would have been only too glad to babble of their adventure, had been bustled quickly into the office and the door closed on outsiders.

A tumble and confusion of voices greeted the sheriff as he answered the summons that brought him striding into the building now. The trio of passengers were doing their talking, and all at the same time, making their complaints to young Ramsey over the disruption of their journey. Ramsey, tie askew and hair rumpled, was having no luck in quieting them; he seemed on the verge of distraction himself, and he turned with a look of instant relief as the door opened under Tyler Gentry's solid hand. The sheriff read and accepted his silent appeal for help, and quickly shouldered into the scene, his heavy bass shearing into the other voices and silencing them: "All right, let's have a little order here!"

The mere voice and size of the man, as well as the awesome authority of the star pinned to his opened vest, had their effect. As stillness settled into the room, he took a flatfooted stand and ran a keen, preliminary glance over the people in it.

Dan Temple was there, leaning back against the partition railing with arms folded and one booted foot hooked across the other, listening without expression. Yonder stood Pearson, the driver, scowling but with an odd secretiveness about him. Stella Ramsey, hands tightly gripping the back of a chair, had gone so white that her eyes were a stain against her face. The other person in the room — the clerk, Becker — showed nothing whatsoever. He was seemingly the only one calm enough to stay seated; he sat hitched back in his swivel chair, toying with a long black penholder, his glance ranging thoughtfully from one to another of the actors in the scene.

Tyler Gentry took this all in, and then matter-of-factly he said, "Now, one at a time! Let's have it! What's the story, Ramsey!"

The young man ran a trembling hand through his hair and started talking. The thing was simple enough to tell; Ramsey had had the facts from Dan and Pearson and he gave them out, in a few broken sentences that showed how worked up he was over this. When he had finished the sheriff cut a sharp glance toward Dan Temple. "Anything to add?"

Dan shook his head. "He's got it the way it happened. The whole thing couldn't have taken more than three or four minutes."

"What about the stickups? You notice anything to identify them if you saw them again?"

"Not much. They were both masked, one shorter than the other — a stocky sort of gent, and strong built. He lifted that express box as though it didn't weigh anything to speak of."

"And the other one?"

Dan's hesitation went without notice. "Nothing at all about him," he lied. "Might have been anybody who's tall and pretty well slimmed down by saddlework."

Gentry said, "Any notion which way they headed when they pulled away from the coach?"

"That would be hard to say. We didn't even see the horses, and hoof sound can fool you."

Tyler Gentry chewed at the inside of his lower lip. "I guess that's it, then," he grunted. "I'll have to get into the saddle!"

One of the drummers spoke up. "I want to know how long we're going to be stuck here. I'm losing money, I tell you!"

"As soon as we can have fresh teams hitched up," young Ramsey assured him impatiently, "the coach will pull out again. I'm sorry about the delay but it couldn't be helped; and it will only mean a couple hours added to the schedule. Now, if you'll just —"

"Boss! Could I talk to you for a minute — alone?"

Everyone looked up at the sudden, blurted question. They were the first words Sim Pearson had spoken for a good many minutes, and they appeared to have burst out of him after some prolonged and silent inner debate. Abel Ramsey, seeing the driver's dark and sombre expression, read something there that made him say, "Why, I — I suppose so." He gestured toward the door of the smaller, private office. "We can go in there, if you got something on your mind —"

"The sheriff, too," muttered Pearson. "I want him in on this." He refused to elaborate, but stood waiting doggedly while his employer turned and exchanged a look with the lawman. The latter shrugged heavily, thin-lipped mouth dragging down, eyes saying it was probably a waste of time. But he nodded, and moved after the others as Ramsey walked to the door and shoved it open. The three of them crossed the threshold and an instant later the door swung silently to behind them.

At once a buzz of wonder over this strange procedure ran through the people in the outer room. Stella Ramsey took a step as though to follow her brother into the other office, and then decided against it; but her white face showed her thoughts.

Only Dan Temple knew what this meant; he had read it in Sim Pearson's whole manner, and in a dozen constrained looks that had passed between the two of them in the interval since the holdup in the hills. Eyes gone suddenly hard, he eased erect from where he had been lounging with his hips against the partition rail. Seeing the shape of things, he all at once knew what had to be done; and without a word, he turned and edged through the swinging gate, moved unobtrusively toward the outer door and, still not hurrying, opened it and stepped out into the sunshine.

The crowd there immediately closed in on him, eager for news, but Dan Temple gave them no attention. He shoved through, and started along the cinder path, his mind on another purpose and on the dangerous turn he saw things taking. He figured how that scene would go, back in the office, and decided he had only a very few minutes. Walking briskly, then, he headed by the shortest route toward the livery stable where his chestnut gelding was stalled.

At the first corner, he nearly rammed into the paunchy figure of John Evans, rounding the building on his hurried way to the stage line office. Evans was without a hat, his thinning hair wind-ruffled, and a look of consternation riding him. Recognizing Temple, the man stopped him with a hand clutching the sleeve of his leather jacket. "What's going on?" he blurted. "What's this about a holdup?" He was panting, breath whistling a little.

Dan Temple pulled free, with irritation. "Ask Ramsey," he said shortly. "You'll find him down at the office."

"They took the payroll?" demanded the mine operator, voice rising as he saw the other start to move away. "You let them make off with the strongbox and all that money — ?"

"I'm afraid," said Temple, "I did." He kept going, not looking back, though he knew the syndicate man was staring after him. Halfway along the next, he turned in under the livery stable sign and entered the cool, booming darkness of the big barn that was redolent with the smell of hay and leather and horses.

His chestnut gelding was in its stall and Dan Temple worked with smooth, quick movements, piling on the blanket and saddle and gear. Despite outward calm, the need for haste plucked at his nerves. He was hurrying, toward the last, as he tightened the latigo and smoothed down the saddle skirt. After that, he led the gelding out into the aisle and there mounted up, ducking his head as he rode under the doorway and down the short ramp into the street.

At once, a shout lifted.

Looking, he saw a number of men rolling up the street, on foot, from the direction of the stage office, and recognized the blocky shape of Sheriff Gentry in the van. The lawman raised an arm and his bass tones carried over the noises of the town: "Temple! Hold on — !"

He waited for no more. Squaring about in

saddle, he kicked with spurless heels and hauled the gelding to the right as it plunged into a quick run, putting him up the street in the opposite direction from the approaching crowd.

Sudden yells were dimmed under the drum of the horse's galloping. In only a matter of seconds Dan Temple had left the last scattered fringe of the little town in the dust behind him; but still he held to a good pace along the stage road, convinced that a pursuit would materialize as soon as Tyler Gentry could find a horse and, perhaps, other men to ride with him.

In a way, this was an almost incredible turn that things had taken. Yet on the other hand he could guess how it must have looked to Sim Pearson, out there at the holdup, and how he must have made it sound in passing it on to Ramsey and the sheriff. If anyone wanted to believe something crooked of Dan Temple, they would not find much in his past to deter them from it.

Well, they couldn't prove their suspicions — that, he was sure of. Whatever Pearson had seen or thought he had seen, there wasn't enough there to go to court with; although on the other hand, he knew he was adding strength to such suspicions by his hurried quitting of town. Nevertheless, he could have done no differently. He had a job ahead of him, now, and staying to face the sheriff didn't figure in his plans for tackling it.

He pushed ahead, therefore, moving fast and straight toward the promising shelter of the hills, knowing that his horse was fresh and that even if he drove it harder now than he should there would be a chance to rest it later. When he glanced back, after a bit, he saw the stain of dust slanting against the lower sky and knew at once that the sheriff had got pursuit under way — and with a good-sized bunch of riders, judging by the smudge they made. He reined down, dropped off the gelding's back a moment and while it blew laid a narrow attention on that dust sign, estimating its distance and speed of travel.

Well, he had several miles on the posse and it was unlikely any of their mounts could make time on the chestnut, so barring a mishap he ought to have little trouble beating them into the hills. There, he thought he could throw them off his trail; moreover, he didn't imagine they would have much incentive to hunt out a trail once lost, there being no clear charge against him and no reward. . . . He gave the cinch a tug and swung up again, sending the chestnut down the next dip in the bunch grass range and pointing dead ahead toward the shelving hills.

A space of hours passed — a tough and sometimes nerve-wracking one, in the course of which he had to admit it had looked, more than once, as though he had cut it too thin and that he was going to lose the gamble. But now, at the end of that time, he pulled up in the shadow of a stand of spruce and, dismounting there, tested the quality of the silence about him with mounting satisfaction.

This was the deep, wild heart of the up-country, rock-ribbed, atangle with thick growth. It was high, here — his breathing and the pumping of his heart knew it. Below this ridge stretched benches and ravines of standing timber, belted with outcrops of red stone. And somewhere down there, he was sure, the sheriff and his makeshift posse had lost him and lost him for good, without much likelihood of stumbling across his trail again if he kept a careful eye out for any signs of danger.

Right now, there was certainly no movement in those lower reaches. The spruce and tall pines stood up, million-spired in the eternal peacefulness of the high hills. Overhead a cloud or two passed majestically, their shadows sweeping and dipping over the lift and fall of the timbered reaches below. A hawk swung and circled on sword-shaped wings, to settle into the timber. Dan Temple watched for some time the place from which the hawk had taken flight, but saw nothing astir there. He settled his mind on that score, and then turned to consider what he had next to do.

He was well above the stage road now, of course, and the point where the holdup had taken place that morning. But he had put a good deal of thought on this thing and it seemed to him highly probable the spade-bearded man and his partner would have climbed, from there. They would want to cross the hills, though likely not by the traveled routes. So, they would head for one of the higher passes, knowing that their trail would cross many bands of the impervious red outcroppings that ribbed these hills and that with each such crossing the chances of pursuit would be by so much lessened. This way, they could take their time and run little risk of stumbling into anything.

Satisfied with his logic, he got into saddle again and struck out on a new course, swinging a wide, slow circle through the upper hills and hunting constantly for sign.

47

Sooner or later, he reasoned, he was bound to cut the trail of the outlaws if only briefly — assuming, of course, that he'd analyzed their thinking soundly.

It was slow going, over steep and treacherous country. The day dragged on toward mid-afternoon. He rode with his leather jacket strapped down behind the cantle, knowing that the instant the sun set and dusk crept out over these heights he would be glad he had it along. For it began to look as though he might be caught out here by nightfall without having picked up the sign he was hunting; that would mean a miserable night of it, and also would mean his quarry getting so many hours ahead of him that he might never catch up.

But then he found the sign, almost passing over it. There were the marks of two horses, climbing out of a rock shelf below him, and fresh. It could only be the stage robbers; moreover, it showed beyond any doubt the very direction of their flight, and toward which of the passes they were headed. Reading all this in a single careful survey of those few shoe prints in the thin soil, Dan Temple at once lifted the reins and sent his gelding forward again, pointing it straight now along his chosen route and not needing to give any more thought or time to hunting sign.

He got up into the pass before the sun set, found the air thin and cold with a few drifted banks of unmelted snow still clinging to the rock. He came out of the pass and began the descent of the western slope with the sun before him, a red swollen ball seen through miles of layered atmosphere. And the last light had not seeped entirely out of the dusk when he discovered that he had reached his goal.

He reined up within a clump of aspen and looked down upon an abandoned mine works — the slag heaps and dark shaft openings, the reduction shed sprawling down the face of the barren slope, a few other scattered and crumbling structures. It was astonishing, really, the bulldog endurance of the men who had once worked this tough up-and-down country for its treasures of gold and silver. A weed-grown cut trail, stretching away by switchbacks and impossible grades to the lower regions beyond, showed how supplies had been got in and the amalgam and crude ore taken out — probably by pack mule train. A terrific undertaking.

But all that had been some year before, and the mine long since abandoned to its ghosts. Therefore, when Dan Temple saw the golden pinprick of light behind a broken window in the main shack, yonder, he knew it could only mean one thing.

Having found the men he was after, he stayed the way he was for a long minute considering. There was no movement about the place. The outlaws must be inside the shack, horses picketed at graze somewhere in the trees below the hideout.

He knew the measure of the man with the spade beard and the agate eyes, but the other made an unknown quantity — one he would have to reckon with. There was, however, no point in trying to slip in unnoticed — nor was it the kind of thing he liked to do. So instead, Dan spoke to his tired gelding and rode straight forward, openly, though with his right hand free and handy to thonged-down holster and jutting gunbutt.

He had gone only a few yards when the light in the shed instantly winked out. Dan kept on. His gelding's irons struck and rang on rock fragments that rattled down the steep hill face as they were dislodged; these sounds heralded his approach, and ceased only as he pulled in a dozen feet from the shed and waited. Silence, somehow eerie and with a ghostlike quality, settled again over the abandoned mine workings. He

50

might have thought he was alone here, but for the light that had been snuffed out at the first hint of his coming.

Then there was the spine-punishing screech of a door being cracked open on sagging hinges, its edge scraping warped floorboards. The voice of the man with the spade beard cut tensely through the stillness: "Yeah?"

Leather creaked as Dan shifted in saddle. He said clearly, "Whoever you're expecting, this isn't him. It's Dan Temple!"

"Temple!" And after another moment: "Who's with you?"

"No one. I came alone, Jackman. I had imagined you'd guess I might show up, after this morning."

"Maybe so." The other's voice was still curt, still suspicious. Now there was a moment in which a hurried, subdued conversation appeared to take place between the two inside the shack, and Dan waited it through. And after the moment had extended itself unconscionably and he was about to call out and prod them with a sharp word, the sibilant whispering broke off; an instant later, a match flared and the dim light steadied again. It showed now the outline of the open door, and the bearded man's silhouette as he shoved it wide.

"All right, Temple. Light down and come in, if you've a mind to. But you can count on it — we'll have a close eye on you!"

Dan edged the gelding nearer, and swung to earth dropping the reins to anchor them. Deliberately he moved toward the door, and Vern Jackman stood aside to let him enter.

The building, Dan thought, must have served once as living quarters for the chiefs of the mining outfit. It had never had much in the way of elegance; now it was a dilapidated ruin of a place, containing a few odds and ends of broken furniture, a couple of box bunks still fastened to the wall, thick layers of dust, cobwebs. An old drum stove, with a graniteware coffeepot set on it, stood in one corner; but the pipe was gone. Smoke from the fire the room's present occupants had burning drifted toward the ceiling venthole as best it could. The only light was a single candle, fastened by its own grease to a plank against the wall.

Temple's nostrils quirked to the sting of drifting wood smoke as he walked into the place, looking about him. "Living in style here, aren't you, Vern?" he said.

The tall man shoved the protesting door closed, put his shoulders against it. He said shortly, "It's a roof," and waited for his visitor to continue.

Seen without a mask, and in the sickly waver of candle flame, Vern Jackman was a gaunt, hollow-jowled figure, his eyes glassy and without any depth at all, but his mouth above the spade beard quirked upward in a tucked-in, secretive smile that made him look as though he enjoyed a private and sardonic jest about life, even in moments when his voice held danger. Oddly contrasted to him was the other man who stood against the opposite wall beneath the candle he had just relighted, scowling at the newcomer.

This one's broad, powerful shape seemed even more foreshortened by the angle of the shadows, and he had a face that was short and wide, with a heavy brow and jaw, a flat nose, narrow eyes, and almost no forehead beneath a close-clipped matting of reddish hair that covered his skull. He eyed the intruder with surly unwelcome, and the stubby, splayed fingers of his right hand rested on a pouched gun as though defying the other to make a wrong move.

Caught between these two, Dan Temple was in a dangerous position and he knew it. He turned quickly, moving back a step or two so as to bring them both within his line of vision. The rickety table came against his hip and stopped him; and then, from this

53

new stand, he suddenly found himself staring directly into the lower of the two box bunks and at the bulging pair of saddlebags dumped there — and the express box lying on its side, empty, its lock broken, on the dusty floor.

He looked away from this, quickly, turning toward the squat shape of the second outlaw as the man snarled, "How'd you find this place, anyway? He must have sold us out! I knew I didn't trust the —"

"Shut up, Monk!" Vern Jackman's voice was crisp, threatening.

Temple recognized the slip, and smiled a little, bleakly. "Nobody sold you out, Monk," he said. "I followed your tracks up here."

"Like hell you did! We didn't leave no tracks."

"I could show you a few you left," said Dan, indifferently.

Vern Jackman's eyes darkened. "Maybe we weren't as careful as we figured. If one man could trail us, others might."

"I left town with a sheriff after me," Dan Temple offered mildly. "I think I shook him off; but you can see for yourself, a man isn't safe to figure that way."

"You mean, you've gone and led a posse in here?" cried Monk, his whole body jerking to his anger.

"That wasn't my intention. As I say, I think I gave them the slip; but I figured I at least ought to warn you."

Vern Jackman put in: "Better get out there, Monk, and watch a spell just to make sure."

"And leave him in here with — that?" Monk jerked his head toward the filled saddlebags on the bunk.

"Get outside!" Jackman's order was sharp. "Give us a signal if you see anything stir."

The other hesitated a fraction of a minute, head thrust forward, eyes boring at his partner as though he would give argument. But what he said was, "If I see anything stir, I'll come back and fix this guy myself!" He shot a threatening glance at Dan Temple and then went shuffling out of the building, his massive arms swinging.

After the door squealed shut they could hear him moving away across the crumbled stones, climbing toward a high point in the slag which the outlaws apparently used for a lookout. The sounds died, there was silence.

"Well, Dan!" said the bearded man, after a little.

"Well, Vern," Temple echoed. "How long has it been? Two years, anyway?"

"All of that." The outlaw came further into the room; he put an elbow on the topmost bunk in the tier and hitched a boot up on the lower one. His toe nudged the filled saddlebags dumped there, but he didn't glance down. "You're looking well." His voice, behind the secret smile, held a note of mockery. "Had lots of sunshine, haven't you?"

"Right now I'm feeling hungry — nothing since breakfast." Temple glanced at the coffeepot steaming on the stove.

"Oh, of course — help yourself! I'll have Monk fry you up some meat, too."

"I wouldn't think of bothering him!" said Dan, with a dry laugh.

A couple of tin cups stood on a shelf beside the stove. He took the one that looked the cleanest, and filled it from the coffeepot. The brew was stout but he preferred it that way. He perched on the edge of the table as he drank, watching his host across the rim of the cup; both men knew that this was but the first, preliminary sparring and they waited cautiously for what would come after.

Vern Jackman dropped his pale eyes to the hands with which Dan held the coffee cup. His V-shaped smile deepened. "Calluses!" he murmured. "The badge of respectability."

"None of those on your hands, are there, Vern?" Temple set the cup on the table beside him, then, straightened a little; for he saw a subtle change in the other's manner.

"Look, fellow!" Jackman's tone was suddenly hard. "Don't lecture me. Not ever! I always kind of liked you, Dan — we seen some tight places together and got out of them together, and for all I know maybe I wouldn't be standing here now except for you. But all that was a long time ago and it's got nothing to do with now, or with the way either of us has gone."

"Still and all," said Dan quietly, "I was kind of disappointed that you'd pick my coach to work, Vern."

"How the hell was I to know?" growled Jackman.

"Don't hand me that! You found out the spot where Pearson always rests his horses, and the exact time we'd be along. It stands to reason you knew who'd be riding shotgun!"

"But I understood —"

Jackman clipped off the words, half spoken; Temple caught them up: "You understood what? That Lawler was to have me bought off?"

The sallow face above the dark, clipped

57

spade beard was at once a mask, expressionless and beyond reading. "And who is Lawler?" murmured Jackman, blandly.

Temple only shot him a wicked grin. Not pursuing the matter, he began to build a cigarette with materials drawn from his shirt pocket. "At that," he went on, "you must have been nearly as surprised as I was, meeting again out there this morning. Still, I noticed you went through with the job. Or, maybe it was Monk wouldn't let you back out of it?" He shoved the cigarette between flat lips, scratched a match on the butt of his sixgun.

The outlaw had dropped his boot from the edge of the bunk, squaring around quickly. He was really angry now, as he snapped: "You think I'm afraid of Monk?" Then, on another thought, the agate eyes narrowed a little. "While we're talking, what about you opening up with that Greener?"

Dan shook his head. "That wasn't me, Vern — it was the other one; the driver. You sort of slipped there, didn't you? Forgetting the shotgun?" He made a face. "I had to pass up an easy chance to grab it, when I threw down the box. Pearson noticed that, and he knew I shoved his arm on purpose when he tried to use the gun himself. He isn't anybody's fool. He told the sheriff —

58

and that's the reason I'm out here in the hills, tonight."

"Oh?" Jackman considered this; then the scowl ironed out of his face and suddenly he was smiling again, smugly. "Well, it's nothing to beef about. You were playing a sucker's game; the hell with it! Now you're here, throw in with the Monk and me. There's this —" He leaned, scooped up the bulging saddlebags. "And there'll be plenty more. Why, it could be the best thing ever happened to you!"

The other seemed to hesitate for just the fraction of an instant, before he shook his head. "No. I've got a stake, Vern. I'm hanging onto it."

"That's foolishness! You'll never be anything but a mugg, Dan. You haven't got the brains for anything but gun-throwing. Why bother to try?"

"Maybe I don't really know," said Dan Temple, his mouth a hard, straight line. "Maybe that's just the kind of a sucker I am." He added, "As things stand now, if I want to save my hide I've got to take what's in those saddlebags and turn it over to the sheriff. That's the reason I followed you up here.

"Toss them over, Vern!"

The gun was in his hand as he finished

59

speaking, the muzzle trained squarely on the other's thin shape. The draw had been so casual, so unexpected, that Jackman was caught staring and unable to make any try for his own weapon. He looked at the gun; he looked at Dan Temple's eyes squinting at him past the film of smoke from the dangling cigarette.

"Right here at my feet, Vern," repeated Dan Temple, waggling the Colt barrel.

A long breath lifted Jackman's gaunt shoulders. "Don't push me too far, Dan," he warned, and his face was ugly. "Don't think, just because we were friends, once —"

Then, getting no response, he shrugged and tossed the heavy bags. They thudded solidly in front of Temple, and Dan nodded. "Good enough. Now I think you'd better turn around."

When the other's back was toward him, he stepped forward, lifted the gun from Jackman's holster and dropped it onto the table. At a further order, and with no other protest, the bearded man stretched out face down upon the lower bunk and Dan made a quick job of tying him, using ropes from the outlaws' saddles that he found, piled in a corner of the room.

Not forgetting that Monk could break in

on this at any moment, he wasted no time beyond making sure the knots were such that Jackman would need time to work loose. As a last precaution, he lifted Jackman's head and slipped the blue neck cloth up over his bearded chin and stuffed it into the man's mouth for a gag. The look of Jackman's agate eyes, when he caught them staring back at him, was utterly beyond fathoming.

Dan Temple straightened. "This should keep you busy for a few minutes, unless Monk comes and turns you loose," he said; and, picking up the saddlebags, he threw them across a shoulder and took a last look at the dim, candlelit room. The express box had been smashed beyond repair in opening it; he gave it a nudge with his boot and decided against burdening himself with the added, unwieldy weight.

He turned away to the door then, pulled it open just enough to slide through. Outside, he moved quickly to his gelding, that still waited on trailing reins, and tossing the saddlebags in place swung lightly up.

Somewhere above him, on the torn slope over the mining sheds, Monk would be keeping watch. Dan Temple didn't look for him. He reined his horse into the forgotten pack trail and sent it forward, pressing the gelding as much as he dared by the uncertain and trickly gleam of starlight. He expected at any moment to hear the lookout's challenge.

CHAPTER FOUR

But apparently Monk was more concerned about a surprise attack from a sheriff's posse than he was in Temple's departure. At the foot of the trail Dan reined back into the bushes and waited, with hand on gunbutt, for some sound from above; he heard none, and so pushed on again through a rock ravine that slanted steeply downward between hill spurs thick with tall-standing pine. Still, he rode carefully.

The night grew older. There would not be any moon, until an hour before dawn, and nothing could be blacker than these deep hills where the lofty trees blanketed what little light the stars might give. Dan Temple kept going, feeling his way; he knew if he worked downward he would eventually pick up one of the trails that threaded the Dragoons, and then he could follow it back across the hump — a better way than trying, blindly, to beat a route for himself toward one of those high, treacherous passes.

It must have been close to midnight when he found a usable trail; perhaps a half-hour later this debouched from a ravine mouth onto a long, silvery ribbon of road that he recognized at once as the stage trace leading west to Antelope. It was a lucky break; he had ridden that road often enough, on shotgun, to be familiar with every twist and turn of it. He placed himself now, knew that he was quite close to the western end of the pass.

The gelding was tired but Dan determined to push on through to Dragoon; if there was a posse looking for him, the quicker he could turn this money over to the sheriff the better it would be for him. Accordingly, he turned up the trace and kept moving, though careful to let the gelding have frequent resting periods.

It was during one of these breathers that he heard the clear, ringing stroke of steel on stone, somewhere below and behind him.

With a muttered oath, Dan Temple quickly sent his horse plunging up the shallow bank and into the black shadow of a tall Engelmann spruce. So he wasn't the only rider on this pass road tonight! His first quick thought, of course, was for the pair at the abandoned mine works, incredible though it seemed that they could have trailed him this far in their desire to recapture the stage loot. Yet, if it were some casual traveler he should have had further sight or sound by this time. Minutes crept by, as he waited with eyes and ears straining against the dark night curtain, and there was nothing. Frowning, he started to wonder if his own imagination could be playing tricks.

He shifted position, nervously. Saddle leather creaked and popped loudly beneath him.

Instantly, in a tangle of brush still further back from the stage road, a gun crashed on the night; lead clipped a spruce branch over Dan Temple's head. He was dropping out of saddle before the echoes thinned, six-shooter sliding into his hand; going to one knee, he let the gun barrel swing in an arc as he waited for another shot and tried to spot the location of his enemy.

He knew now what had happened. Guessing that he had been overheard and that his quarry would have drawn off the road to wait, the trailer had dismounted and left it also, to start a circle through the brush and so draw in from an unexpected angle. He was up there now, above Temple, probably bellying the needle-littered earth and trying to make up his mind whether the first shot had tallied.

Limbs cramping beneath him, Dan Temple shifted slightly; he felt the pull of taut nerves, felt the chill touch of the night upon face and hands that were suddenly beaded with sweat. He had no taste for such work as this. He laid his gun across a bent thigh, rubbed his palm against the tight-stretched denim of his pantleg to scrub the moisture from it. Then, taking the gun again, he reached with his other hand and began to feel of the earth in a widening circle about the spot where he crouched.

After a moment he found what he wanted; his fingers closed upon the damp round of a windfall — a short length of limb, thick and fairly heavy. He picked it up carefully, balancing the heft of it, and straightened to a stand. Then, with a sharp jerk of the arm, he suddenly sent that chunk of wood spinning, end for end, far into the brush to one side of him.

As it crashed into the growth, the man on the bank above him rose to the bait. Red fire straked from up there — once, twice, directed at the false sound. And then Temple's own sixshooter was working and he was lunging straight up the tricky rise of ground, triggering as he went.

Quickly, the other switched to this new target and his next bullet sang close to

Temple's bent, running form. Dan kept going, lifting his feet high to avoid being tripped by tangling growth as he closed the distance. The two sixguns were in point-blank range now; they blended their thunder, stabbed at the darkness with streaks of muzzle flame. A moment, only. Then, a sudden, choked scream tore from the shadows ahead; the opposing gun fell quickly silent.

Dan Temple held off the trigger, stood there at a crouch with senses numbed by racket and gunflare, and heard the thrashing in the brush die with the fading echoes. It could be a trick, though he doubted it; he waited out another twenty seconds to be sure. Then he moved forward, carefully, and halted only when his toe met the yielding sprawl of a body on the ground.

He knew the man was dead, just from the way he gave to the prodding. The contact filled him with a kind of nausea and he jerked his foot back, hastily. Only then did he slide the smoking, nearly empty gun back into his holster; and only then did he become conscious of the fact that he himself was bleeding.

It slid down his ribs, a slow trickle of warm wetness, underneath his right arm. He hadn't known when the bullet struck, and he felt little pain even now. The exploring fingers of his left hand found where the lead had sliced him, just below the armpit — the smallest of scratches. He winced a little as he probed the spot. But it was of no importance; and reaching into a pocket he fumbled out a match and, bending forward, snapped it alight upon his thumbnail. The flickering, unsteady flame picked out the brutish, dead features of the man named Monk — his eyes staring and sightless, his throat a bloody mess where the bullet had ripped it open.

So that was that. But what of Vern Jackman?

Even in revulsion at the ugliness of death, Temple found it in him to be glad it was Monk and not his one-time friend that he had killed. But was Jackman out there in the night somewhere, ready to make his try at Temple now that Monk had lost? The thought made him drop the still-burning match hastily and set a boot upon it. In the returned darkness, he crouched near Monk's corpse and told himself that if there had been more than one of them he would have drawn fire from Jackman before this.

So he straightened, feeling the tautness of danger and battle slide away from him. And he turned and went down the slope toward the road, and the tall spruce near which his gelding still stood on trailing reins, holding its place in spite of near-by gunfire. He saw the shape of the horse, dimly; saw it shy away with mincing steps and a nervous tossing of the head as he approached, and should have taken warning from that. Instead he murmured, "Sho' — sho' now!" and reached to take the reins.

"All right!" It was the heavy bass of Sheriff Gentry, from directly behind him. "Stand fast, Temple, and up your hands! We'll take no foolishness from you!"

Astonishment swamped every other reaction. Dan stiffened, turned slowly to face the blocky shape of the lawman as Gentry came wading forward now out of the shadows. Suddenly, he found that he was surrounded, where a moment ago there had seemed to be only the emptiness of the night. The forms of men closed in upon him. Someone grunted, "Bring up that lantern. Who's got it?"

The spot of a bull's-eye speared across the scene. There were a half dozen in the posse, their faces grim and wicked-looking in the lantern glow, that showed also the glint of the guns they carried. Looking about, Dan Temple saw they were all men that he knew; he was more than a little surprised to discover Abel Ramsey himself,

68

among the rest.

Sheriff Gentry bawled orders: "A couple of you go up and see if you can find what's left of the other one. He's likely dead." As those two hurried away, he added to Temple, "A lucky break for us, though not for you. Trailing is poor business in these hills, at night. We would have turned back in another minute except we heard the shots. Had a falling out, did you?"

Temple blinked. He started to exclaim, "Now, wait a minute! Don't make any wrong guesses!" But he was cut off by a shout as one of the men, for the first time, spotted the saddlebags slung across behind the gelding's saddle. Young Ramsey shouldered his way forward, then, seized the pouches and fumbled at the flaps with trembling hands.

"It's here!" he cried, hoarsely. "This is the Yellow Jack shipment, all right!"

"Good!" grunted the sheriff. "A fair night's work. The loot, and one of the crooks dead, and another — the one we wanted the worst — ready for a cell!" His eyes pinned on Temple's tight features, he reached out and deftly plucked the reeking gun from the prisoner's holster.

Dan let it go. A cold numbness was knotting inside him as he saw the shape this was taking. "I tell you, you've got the thing wrong!" he said, flatly. "I took the money away from the holdups and had to kill one of them doing it. I was just bringing it back to turn it in!"

"That's very likely!" said the sheriff. His face held no change of expression, but his voice was heavy with scorn.

And then a hand seized Temple and hauled him around forcibly so that he had to fight for balance; and Abel Ramsey glared at him in the weird light of the bull's-eye. "You filthy swine!" Ramsey's mouth worked over the vileness of the words he spoke. "You damned, weasel-hearted renegade! To think I let you fool me into believing you could go honest and stay that way —"

Face gone white, Dan Temple said sharply, "Watch your tongue, Ramsey!"

Ramsey hit him. There wasn't much steam behind the wild swing but it splatted square into the center of Dan's face and it stung. With a roar of insulted pride Dan Temple started for him then; but two men caught his arms and despite the sudden blind fury that drove him he could not tear loose. They hauled him back, and it felt almost as though they would screw his arms out of the sockets before he subsided; hat gone, hair streaming into his face, he stood with their hands firm upon him and his eyes sought the one who had struck him.

He saw quick fear in Abel Ramsey, at the storm his words and his blow had nearly unleashed. The man faded back a little, mouth working, hands half-raised as though he thought Temple might still get at him. And Temple put all his own loathing into a contemptuous silent stare.

"Enough of this!" said Tyler Gentry, in a crisp voice. The sudden violence had raised a babble of excitement but it died out under his firm command; and now the two he had dispatched up the hill were coming back, grunting a little under the weight of what they carried between them.

"He's dead enough," one of them announced. "A stocky, heavy-built gent — sounds like the description all right."

Somebody said, "What about the other one? There was two held up the stage."

Gentry looked at his prisoner. "Got anything to say?"

Gone stubborn, sullen, Dan Temple flicked him a sour glance. "Nothing!"

"All right — suit yourself!" The sheriff turned to his men. "We've done well enough — we'll settle for this much, and head back. Get the horses." He nudged with a boot toe

71

the lifeless shape of the dead man. "This thing must have left a bronc somewhere. See if you can find it, and bring 'em both in. Meanwhile, we'll go on ahead and put the other one into cold storage where he belongs. . . ."

. . . And thus they brought Dan Temple back to Dragoon, the center of a grim and silent calvalcade. It was close to dawn when they clattered into the sleeping streets; the first cold gray of daylight was already staining the air by the time preliminaries of booking him had been accomplished, and Sheriff Gentry led him down to the cell-block in the courthouse basement and locked him into one of the bleak, narrow rooms of steel.

Dan Temple had little to say during all this, because he had said what he could already and not been believed. The sheriff's solid stride echoed into the distance and somewhere at the head of iron-treaded stairs another door clanged shut, closing him away there with silence and his own dour thoughts. For some moments, Temple stood peering between strap-iron bars into the dim corridor. A drunk was sleeping off a jag in a cell across from him; otherwise, Temple was the only prisoner. It was the first time he had ever seen the inside of a jail.

He turned, after a bit, and crossed the damp concrete flooring and stretched out on the hard bunk, hands under his head, to look up at a single high window and the lightening sky beyond. He was dead-beat from hours in the saddle, shaky from the emptiness of his belly. Yet, too drugged with tiredness for sleep to take hold and release him quickly, he could only lie there and brood upon the spot that he was in and the sour outlook for the future.

He would get in a lawyer this morning sometime, of course — Dragoon boasted two of them, one a boozy old wreck who had been a notorious hanging judge in his prime, the other an incompetent youngster just out of school. But the best lawyer could do little good, against his own reputation and the prejudice that that reputation had raised against him. Dan saw as much, with a sudden bleak clarity. He saw all at once that there was no one who could help him now — and he couldn't think, in that moment, of anyone who would even be willing to try . . .

Old Tom McNeil shifted his bones in the saddle and threw a sardonic look at his companion. "Well, Ruth," he said. "I reckon this is about where it happened. Now maybe

73

you'll tell me what you think you can do, since we're here?"

"Oh, damn it, how do I know what we can do?" The girl looked about her helplessly, at the sunbright pine and spruce and the rugged land that climbed about them, up to the high and windy pass over which they had just come following the tortuous loopings of the stage trace. She clenched a small brown fist upon the horn of her saddle, let it fall open again. "You sure this is the place, Tom?" Her tone was dubious and without hope.

The old cowpuncher shrugged hunched shoulders. "I reckon I'm sure. See them marks?" His rope-scarred hand pointed to the dust at their horses' feet. "A lot of riders stirred that up. And, yonder —" He swung his arm toward the scrubby slope above the road. "That's where the shootin' must have been, and where they grabbed him. Now, then," he grumbled, "if'n you've seen what you come all this crazy distance to look at, maybe we can start back. I'm gonna be laid up, I can tell, bustin' these hills in a saddle for so many hours, and at my age. What's more, your dad will likely fire me if he learns I been helpin' you waste your time like this for that nogood Dan Temple!"

She wanted to make him a sharp answer, but the words were caught in the sudden swelling within her throat and she could say nothing at all for a moment; then it was to ask him, in a tone that was as near to pleading as she had ever come: "Won't you stick by me, Tom? You got to! I — I dunno what chance there is to help Dan and prove the things they say about him aren't so. But maybe there's something —"

"Your eyes are as sharp as they ever were, Tom, and I know you can read sign like an Indian. Help me now. What do the tracks say?"

"Likely nothin'," he grunted. "If that fool posse left anything that's not too smeared up to read. This is a crazy notion, girl!" But he had been challenged in the one art to which he laid especial claim, and his self-esteem had been touched by her faith in his ability. So, despite distaste for the purpose to which he was working, he gave it now his reluctant attention.

Mumbling to himself, he tugged the battered hat lower over his furrowed brow and under the brim's shade squinted at the ground. Ruth watched him, frowning with concern but not daring to speak. Overhead the noon sun was warm, despite the early season and the altitude; a slight breeze came down the heights, tugging at her hair and ballooning the white blouse she wore above her beaded riding skirt. Ruth noticed neither breeze nor sun, her anxious glance following old Tom without any real hope that the man could accomplish anything.

McNeil rubbed the warped knuckles of a crumpled, rheumatic hand across the gray stubble on his toothless jaw. "We-ell," he observed, as though he were about to offer a statement, and then, instead, fell silent.

After another moment of this he nudged his sorrel mare and began moving down the road at a slow walk, away from the pass, while he leaned far out of saddle studying the marks he found in the dust. He went clear down over the curve of the hill and out of sight there, hidden by the scrub growth that lined the road.

Ruth wanted to follow but feared to obliterate any of the sign; so she stayed where she was, waiting. It seemed a long time indeed before Tom came back into view, still walking the mare, her head bobbing as she took the climb. Not even looking at the girl, Tom rode past and then, pulling the mare aside suddenly, put her up the shallow roadbank and halted beneath a tall, slim-bodied Engelmann. Here he dismounted, squatted down and took a careful reading.

He lifted his head, shot a long, speculative glance at the slope above him, the brush that wavered in the rising wind. At last he straightened, with a grimace of pain for creaking joints.

"Well, this is where Temple left his bronc, all right," he said finally, returning to the waiting girl. "Under this big spruce. He was riding up the trail when —"

"*Up* the trail?" she broke in, sharply. "Wait a minute! Are you sure of that, Tom? He was really heading back toward Dragoon — with the money?"

"I got eyes, ain't I?" he retorted. "Look for yourself! Here's the sign the posse made, comin' over the pass. And yonder, there's tracks of Temple's gelding — pointin' from the other direction."

"But doesn't that prove — ?"

"Also," he went on, not letting her interrupt, "two-three hundred yards downslope there's overlapping prints of a second bronc follerin' Temple's — at a good clip, too, judging from the length of the stride. There's a stone imbedded in the trail, has the scrape of the iron on it; and that noise must have carried quite a distance. It must have been what gave Temple warning and drove him into cover.

"Meantime, of course, the other fellow knew he'd given himself away. He left his mount, groundhitched; I found the gouge of his bootmarks in the shoulder of the road and followed them. He circled through the brush, worked in above Temple and jumped him. That's when they had their fight — and this other guy got killed!"

Ruth Chess had listened, enthralled, to the old man's reading of the story from a handful of obscure marks in the dust of a road. As Tom McNeil finished she leaned from the saddle and seized his arm, gripping the spare and bony elbow hard through the faded cloth of his shirt.

"You're — you're wonderful!" she breathed. "To be able to tell all that. Just as if you'd been here last night and seen it happen —"

He made a deprecatory gesture. "Hell, there ain't much you can do with sign as old as this here. Wind's blown a lot of it away, and that stupid posse trampin' back and forth ain't helped a mite. Still, anybody with a pair of eyes could have told what I have — if he'd just take the trouble to use them!"

"Don't be so modest! There's not another man in the county can pair you reading sign. . . . But the important thing is, you've cleared Dan! You've shown he couldn't possibly have been meaning to keep the money for himself. Because, he knew these hills were full of the sheriff's men; he wouldn't have dared to risk riding the stage road with the loot in his saddlebags — unless he was bringing it back to turn it in! Don't you see?"

"Yeah, I see all right." Yet the girl sensed something in Tom McNeil's manner that caused her to turn a sharp look on him.

"What's the matter, Tom?"

The scowl deepened on his weathered face as he swung away, pegged over to his sorrel mare. Fumbling with the cinch, he growled:

"I was just thinkin' it's too bad I ain't got it in me to keep my mouth shut, and let what will happen to that fellow! He's where he deserves to be, more'n likely — even though he wasn't guilty of this particular charge . . ."

"Why, that's not true! Dan may have been kind of wild, in the old days, but even so there was never any talk of crookedness made about him — not until this thing came up. You know that, as well as I do; the trouble is, you're prejudiced against him!"

"All right," the old puncher admitted, grudgingly. "And suppose I am! I also know that you're in love with the guy — and do you think he'll even say 'thanks' for the trouble you've taken?" McNeil added, with bitter humor. "At most, he'll say it was *neighborly* of you!"

She felt the barb, but she said only, "I'd have done the same for any innocent man in trouble. And I'm not worried about your holding back what you've discovered, even if it does mean helping Dan Temple. You're too honorable a man, Tom!"

"Yeah, ain't it a fact?" muttered Tom McNeil, darkly, shoving a worn boot toe into stirrup. "I'm too holy to live. . . ."

When Sheriff Gentry came down to the cellblock, Dan Temple was in conference with his lawyer, "Judge" Homer — an untidy, tobacco-stained derelict whose nickname and faintly legal air were all that remained of his former standing as a jurist. Dan had been pacing the damp and chilly cell while Homer perched on the edge of the bunk, shaking his head at the story the prisoner told him. As Dan finished, the untidy old man leaned forward, spat brown juice onto the concrete and then smeared it there under the firm sole of one high-button shoe.

"You ain't got a chance!" he pronounced flatly. "Was I trying your case, I'd give you the limit. As it is, I don't think I'd care

80

about representin' you. Better send for that whipper-snapper in the office across the street from mine — not that he can do you any good, either."

"I'd as soon stand my own defense," said Temple, coldly.

It was then that the solid, flatfooted stride of the sheriff came echoing along the corridor and Gentry stabbed a key into the lock of the cell door.

"Temple!" he barked. "Step over here!"

Dan obeyed, scowling. "Now what?"

"Some questions I want to ask you. That is, if you're ready to answer 'em yet!"

"I am," replied Temple, "any time you're ready to hear me without making your mind up in advance that I'm guilty!"

Tyler Gentry had a troubled look about him, like that of a man who has heard news which upsets his preconceptions. He said, heavily, "Well, and I'm listening. . . . I'd like you to tell me, Temple, just why you ran out on me yesterday afternoon."

Dan said, "I had good reason. Sim Pearson's not hard to read. I knew he had a notion about that stickup and that he was going to sic you on me. And since I figured I was responsible for the loss of the money I meant to have a chance at getting it back."

Gentry considered this answer, his scowl

pinned on the other. "So you went into the hills, and you found the outlaws — when I and my men were hunting all over the place without a sign of them!"

"I played in luck."

"And, singlehanded, you braced the pair of 'em and got the money? And let the crooks go without even trying to capture them?"

Dan shrugged. "I'm no badge-toter, Gentry. It was the money I went after."

The sheriff scraped a thoughtful knuckle across his jaw. "You know that story has got holes in it, don't you?" he muttered darkly. "Holes I could drive a team and wagon through!"

"But the fact remains, I brought the loot back with me — and I killed one of the crooks when he followed and tried to stop me from doing it. You can't make a crook out of me, Sheriff, until you explain *that* away."

Gentry nodded, slowly. "Yeah," he admitted, "that's the one thing I can't get around. Because the evidence shows now that you really were bringin' it back — and that spoils my whole case. After all, I got nothin' but Pearson's story. And he was only guessin'. . . . But one more question:

"Exactly what was it, Temple, gave you

wind of the fact that this galoot you killed was fixing to jump you?"

Dan Temple frowned. "Why, it was a simple thing. I heard a noise. I heard his bronc's iron strike against a rock —"

The sheriff released his breath, then, in a grunt. The key in his hand twisted; the lock clicked open. "All right," he muttered, swinging the door wide. "Ramsey says to drop charges and I guess that's that. Step out, fellow. You're cleared!"

The whole affair was a little past Dan's comprehension, but he felt no urging to argue the matter. He cocked a glance at Judge Homer and his mouth twisted sardonically.

"Thanks for the legal advice, fellow," he said, drily. "It proved very helpful and interesting."

Afterwards he turned and went past Tyler Gentry, and the old man on the cot hitched to his feet and followed them out into the corridor, shaking his whiskered head over this strange reversal of justice.

In the office at the head of the clanging iron steps, Gentry turned Dan over to a deputy who handed him the sealed manila envelope containing his personal belongings, and took Dan's belt and gun out of a drawer and passed them over. Temple accepted these with no comment and a brief nod of thanks.

He strapped the weapon in place, dragged on his hat, and left.

Outside, in the dim hallway that split the building from front to rear, three men stood silhouetted against the smear of sunlight beyond the wide-open entrance of the courthouse. They turned quickly as Dan Temple appeared.

One of the three was Tyler Gentry; the others, Abel Ramsey and — surprisingly enough — Tom McNeil. Dan gave the old puncher a questioning glance, wondering what the man was doing here, and got a flinty look in answer. Then he forgot McNeil as Abel Ramsey cleared his throat and switched Dan's attention.

Ramsey seemed to be having trouble finding what he wanted to say. "Well, Temple," he began, and hesitated as though he expected the other man to help him out. There was no help coming from Dan Temple. He stood where he was, flatfooted, and stared at Ramsey; and a core of hot anger had started to smolder and to grow inside of him. Suddenly his bruised jaw, under its day-old growth of beard stubble, began to sting to the memory of Ramsey's fist smashing against it.

But Ramsey seemed not to know what was going on within the other man. He blundered ahead with his speech, not choosing his words too well, and unaware of the effect they might have. "There's been a little — mistake, I guess. We're convinced now that you really intended bringing that stolen money back; and at any rate, we do have the money and one of the thieves is dead. So we'll let it go at that, and no more questions asked. Everything will be as it was. Is that agreed?"

Unconsciously Dan Temple's fists, hanging at his sides, were working, curling and unclosing, as in his mind he heard again the other words that this man had said to him last night. *You filthy swine! . . . To think I let you fool me into believing you could go honest and stay that way!* He stood looking at Ramsey with that remembered, raging voice within his head, and his eyes were ice-gray and a small pulse had started leaping in his set jaw.

Ramsey frowned, a little, getting no answer. "Well, I'm waiting, Temple! Are you going back to work for me? Are we going to forget everything that's happened?"

. . . damned, weasel-hearted renegade . . . filthy swine.

Sheriff Gentry said in his heavy bass,

"Speak up, man! What's your answer?"

Shoulders lifting then as he drew a long breath into lungs that suddenly felt cramped, Dan Temple's head jerked sharply. "My answer? All right, here it is: We aren't going to forget it! Not quite as fast as you'd like. It isn't that simple, Ramsey!"

The face of his former employer lost color slowly as Temple's words stung home. "You used talk to me last night," said Dan, "that I've never taken from any man yet. What's more, you used your fists, when I didn't have a chance to get back at you! And you expect me to forget that? You think a man's pride counts for nothing?"

He reached out, quickly, and Ramsey stammered something and tried to back clear. But Temple didn't hit him; instead, he jerked open the front of Abel Ramsey's suitcoat and revealed, as he had expected, that there was no weapon strapped to the man's soft middle. He dropped his hand, let the suitcoat fall back into place.

"Next time we meet," he said, spacing the words like missiles thrown into the other's white and frightened face, "you be packing a gun!"

And leaving that challenge in the shocked stillness of the hallway, he heeled about and strode out of the courthouse. No sound but the pound of his own footsteps followed him.

CHAPTER FIVE

Toward seven, Temple came down from his room at the hotel, still in a dangerous mood though rested and feeling better for the chance to shave and clean up from the stench of the damp cellblock. When he crossed the lobby into the dining room, he sensed the quick stir his entrance caused. But no man in that room met his eye directly, as he stood in the fringed doorway, and surveyed the scatter of tables.

Yonder, the clerk, Paul Becker, had pushed back his chair and risen to leave just as Dan entered. He hesitated momentarily, as though reluctant to meet face to face with Temple as he would have to do. But there was something that had to be said and the latter stayed where he was, blocking the door, giving him no choice. Becker came along the carpet strip, moving stiffly, and he halted when Temple spoke.

"Seen your boss?"

"No." The reply was curt, stony; Becker's eyes were dark with more than their usual hostility, but there was also a hint of fear in them.

Temple said, "I'll be in the hotel bar at nine tonight. You tell him that."

"I'm not your messenger."

"I said, tell him!"

Dan Temple made no real effort to keep the contempt out of his voice. The clerk, with his Eastern manners and his hands whose only calluses were those at the first joints of the two fingers that held a steel-nib bookkeeper's pen, was to him a person out of his setting in this tough land — a mockery of the large, strong-bodied men who were its natural product. He glared his open hatred of Temple now; his narrow shoulders lifted. But afterwards, without answering, he whipped past and moved through the archway and across the lobby beyond.

Dan turned back to meet again the intent stares of the room. He was sure his message to Ramsey had been overheard. Long before nine o'clock, the whole town would know of it.

He had his meal; full night was come when he went out into the street. The town seemed strangely silent. The chill darkness felt clean upon his skin, but it seemed to Dan he could still smell the sour, faintly mildewed dampness of the cellblock.

Despite his words to Becker, harsh distaste for this entire business sat strongly upon him. Having, in a quick break of savage temper, made his challenge to Abel Ramsey, his narrow code could offer him no loophole now to escape its consequences. Dan Temple didn't want that meeting at nine o'clock; he took no pleasure in the thought of pitting himself against a weakling such as Ramsey. Yet pride, and the stern logic of events, gave no other out, left him no alternative.

He stepped into a dingy tobacco shop and pool room combination, bought a cue and began working off his mood by knocking the ivory balls around a table, sinking tricky shots, scowling darkly as he squinted along his polished cue stick. He was the only man in the place, besides the proprietor; the sharp strike of cue tip against ivory, the roll of the balls across the felt, were startlingly loud in the stuffy silence.

But presently, as he leaned to gauge a shot into the far pocket of the table, Dan became suddenly conscious of someone standing at his elbow. He sank the shot before he straightened, turning, and saw Reed Lawler nodding and smiling at him, the white teeth gleaming in smoky lamplight.

"Very nice," said the big man. "A steady hand — a good eye."

Lawler had a cue of his own and he was

chalking it briskly. Temple supposed if he hadn't been so engrossed in what he was doing he would have noticed the other's entrance. He grounded the butt end of his stick, leaned both hands on it as he regarded the other levelly beneath the cone of light from the ceiling-hung, shaded lamp above the table. He saw that the man's mouth was still swollen and discolored from the blow Temple's fist had dealt him, two nights ago.

"Shall we play for a few points?" Reed Lawler suggested pleasantly.

Temple answered bluntly, "I don't think I want to. Just killing a little time."

"Suit yourself." But the big man stayed where he was, working with the chalk and eyeing Temple with a half-smile on his block features. Dan turned his back, fished the ball he had just sunk out of the table pocket and spun it idly across the felt. He got his cue ball and tossed it reflectively in one palm as he walked around the table hunting an interesting lie to shoot into.

Reed Lawler said abruptly, "Have you thought any more about my proposition?"

Slowly, Temple straightened up, resting his cue across the table edge. His eye was stony. "Yes," he said, "I've thought about it. I'm thinking I let you off easy, with only one clout in the jaw!"

"You were just lucky!" the big man retorted, reddening a little as anger broke briefly through the calm of his exterior. "You caught me off guard or it wouldn't have turned out that way." He tossed the chalk aside, slapped the cue tip into a big palm a time or two; after that he had control again and he said, in a different tone, "I meant what I said, that night; I still mean it. I'd like you to go to work for me."

"Doing what?" rejoined Temple, unbending. "Taking Monk's place?"

Lawler's broad face went carefully blank. "You talk riddles."

"Maybe. But I think you know the answers to them."

"I don't, though. I offered to beat Ramsey's pay if you'd quit him and ride shotgun for me. Well, I see you've left Great Western; I'm still offering to hire you now if you want to come on my payroll."

"I wouldn't know what for," said Temple, looking squarely at him. "Unless you need someone to hold Jackman in line and keep him off the wrong stages. And after our little trouble at the mine last night, I don't imagine he'd take kindly to the idea. He didn't like it a bit when I walked out with the saddlebags."

Coldly, Lawler said, "Really, I don't make

sense out of a word you're saying! I never heard of this Jackman, or Monk, either one."

Temple knew he was lying. He merely shrugged and, turning back to the game, made a deliberate shot and sent the balls clicking and shuttling under the cone of smoky light. But Reed Lawler continued, unperturbed:

"I'm going into competition with Great Western. The plans I mentioned two nights ago are set; I've leased a building and tomorrow work crews will start putting up barns and fencing in a wagon yard. Two coaches and a line of freight wagons are already on the way here, and I've sent a man into the field to buy up horses and mules. I told you before, there's money behind this thing — it's no fly-by-night proposition. And it isn't too late for you to come in, if you want to find a place in it — now that you and the Ramseys are definitely split. . . ."

Slowly Dan lifted his glance from the table. A dangerous light danced at the back of his eyes as he said quietly, "How much does it take to convince you, Lawler, that a man's no means 'no'?"

Reed Lawler must have sensed the danger in that softly spoken question. He lost a little of his easy self-assurance; the color ebbed a bit in his florid, virile features and he even retreated a step, involuntarily.

In that one moment, Dan Temple read a flicker of fear in the man which he had not seen in him before. But for a moment only; then the brazen front that Lawler kept up to the world slid back and covered this single hint of weakness. The mouth twisted again into its habitual, amused smirking.

"I forgot," he murmured. "I keep giving you credit for intelligence, and you keep disappointing me. Well, I won't make that mistake again, Temple!"

He turned away abruptly. Dan Temple watched the blocky figure as Reed Lawler moved unhurriedly across the room, racked his cue, and left the place without a backward glance. Frowning, Dan thought with a certain hard pleasure: He covered up quick, but I think I had him scared. . . .

It was just then that the banjo clock on the wall began to strike the hour. Nine.

Quickly he straightened, as at a summons. The old man behind the counter lowered his newspaper. He said, through the thin beat of the strokes, "That clock's five minutes fast, Temple. You don't need to hurry —"

But Dan had already tossed his cue onto the table top, and was striding for the door

93

with the old man's hard glance following him. Temple didn't see the old man throw down his paper, as the door slammed, blow out the lamp above the counter and hobble quickly after him, leaving the other lamps burning in his anxiety not to miss anything. . . .

The dark streets with their occasional splashings of light from door and window were as deserted as they had been earlier in the evening. The deadness of things about this town tonight was not unusual, of course, for the middle of a working week; it did not at all prepare Dan Temple for what he found when he pushed through the side door of the hotel bar and came into the big, brightly lighted room.

It was nearly full. Hard to say where all these men had come from but they were here, and not for the purpose of drinking. A few, indeed, had bar glasses in their hands but they appeared to have forgotten them; over all there seemed the atmosphere more of waiting, or of a wake.

Some of the men were townspeople, others punchers from out on the near-by spreads. They all showed a kind of sheepishness, as though each knew why the others were there and was a little ashamed of being there for the same reason. But nobody ventured to leave; and as the door slammed under Temple's heel and those nearest turned to see who had entered, an instant awareness seemed to run through everyone in the place and every head turned toward the newcomer. A kind of suffocated stillness fell upon the stuffy room.

Dan Temple walked into this cottony silence, not giving more than a glance to any face about him, and moved directly to the bar. A space cleared for him there and he settled an elbow against the wood, nodded to the man in the green-striped shirt for a glass and bottle to be set in front of him. He filled the glass, set the bottle carefully to one side. Lifting the drink, he looked across the sparkling rim of it and saw his own reflection in the back bar, and the medley of expressions on the faces around him, all intently watching him.

There was a clock here, too. Its hands pointed exactly on nine; and this gave him the odd sensation of time having stood still as he walked the chill block from the pool-hall, where that other clock had showed precisely the same face to him as he left.

Temple tossed off the whiskey, put the empty glass aside. Turning, then, he saw the crowd shifting apart as someone came directly toward him, and he squared about, right hand dropping quickly to hang near the tied-down holster. But he was not particularly surprised when he saw that this was not Abel Ramsey, but the sheriff.

Gentry shouldered into a place next to Temple and faced him squarely, his expressive eyes bitter, his mouth a thin-lipped, grim line. He said, without preamble, "So you're going through with this! I see you brought out quite a crowd for it, too."

Dan flicked a glance about the room, returned it to the sheriff. He said briefly, "Every man's got the right to take a drink."

"You know what I'm talking about!" muttered the lawman. He added, "I ain't sure but what I ought to put you back into that cell — *before* you kill Ramsey!"

"Look," said Dan, coldly. "Abel knows I'm to be here at nine o'clock. He doesn't have to come; but if he does it's his own free will, and no business for you, Sheriff!"

"You'll murder him! Abel Ramsey ain't any match for you."

"I won't draw first, Sheriff."

"It will still be murder!" said Gentry. "As far as I'm concerned, it will. Better keep it in mind that I warned you."

"So that's how it is?" Dan considered the other narrowly. "I don't think I like your kind of justice, Gentry," he said finally. "According to you, I'm supposed to let a man throw any kind of talk he wants to at me, and then have me tossed into that stinking jail of yours on no evidence at all. Is that your idea?"

The sheriff spread a palm. "Ramsey was out of his head last night — too worked up to know what he was doing."

"I suppose that excuses him?" Temple looked past the lawman's grizzled head then, at the clock above the bar. His mouth quirked. "Well, I guess your friend is using his head tonight, all right. It's ten after. He's not coming."

Gentry, in turn, looked at the face of the clock. Then he swiveled and ran a frowning glance toward each of the bar's three exits — to the hotel lobby, to the veranda at the front, to the side street beyond the counter. Temple thought he saw the shadow of disappointment across the man's eyes, as Gentry had to admit that Dan was probably right and that Ramsey had passed up the challenge, lacking the nerve to meet it. But the sheriff banished this with a shrug. He said, loyally, "Abel's no fool."

"Maybe not — but he's sure as hell yellow!" snapped Temple. And digging into a pocket he slapped silver onto the bar to pay for his drink, and started for the veranda doorway.

Behind him, the sheriff snapped, "Where you going?"

"Why, could be I'm going hunting for him," retorted the other, across a shoulder, and went out of there before the sheriff had time to say more.

A kind of buzzing was abroad in the bar now, as the men who had gathered for the showdown between Temple and his former boss realized that it was not going to come off, after all. Dan knew they had been hoping for the sight of blood — anyone's blood. He was glad when the door closed behind him and the whiskey smell and the rasping voices were shut away.

On the cinder path before the hotel, he halted for a deep breath of cleaner air. A tension had suddenly lifted from him. As far as he was concerned the thing was settled, the point of honor satisfied; he had come through a bad situation in not too disagreeable a fashion. As for Ramsey, his feelings toward the man had damped down and settled into a kind of sullen contempt. The whole thing now was a matter best forgotten. . . .

A man edged up to him out of the shadows. "Temple?"

Dan turned quickly. He recognized the

shapeless, stubble-bearded features. This was one of the habitual loafers who hung around the company's stables, doing occasional odd laboring jobs for the price of a drink or a meal. The reek of cheap whiskey and stale dirt came from him as he sidled nearer, with a hoarse and confidential whisper.

"If you want Ramsey, you won't find him. He saddled a bronc and left town three quarters of an hour ago. In a hell of a hurry, too! I seen him leave." The bum waited, showing his teeth in a crooked grin.

But Temple had taken this news almost without hearing it, since it meant nothing to him now. "All right," he said, absently. And he started to move away.

"I thought you'd want to know, Mr. Temple." The voice of the man in the shadows rose to a whine. "I went out of my way to tell you. It wasn't nothing I had to do —"

With a grunt of distaste, Temple halted long enough to fish out a dollar and fling it to him, and watch him grab it from the air, babbling thanks. And he thought, in a thickening flash of revelation: *That's* working for wages! That's groveling for whatever another man wants to throw to you. . . . I'm through with it! The hell with them all —

the Ramseys, and Reed Lawler too. I'll go out to that place of mine and I'll build it from my own sweat. Maybe I'll starve, but I'll be my own man. . . .

And with this resolve putting a new and solid quickness into him, he moved back up the steps and across the hotel lobby, hurrying as he climbed to the second floor. Despite the lateness of the hour, he was suddenly all eagerness to get his saddleroll together, check out of this town and take the trail to his ranch. It was the first wholehearted decision he had made in many weeks; the burden of an onerous, dragging job had lifted from him and though it left him with pockets virtually empty it sent a warmth flooding through him at the same time.

Freedom! That was what he had thrown away when he took on the onus of respectability and with it the grinding toil of two full-time jobs. There would still be toil enough, on his homestead section at the springs; but it would be at his own dictation and to his own use, with no other man to order him or profit from his efforts.

So thinking, on a note of quiet exultation, he reached his own door toward the far end of the carpeted, lamplit hallway. It had been left unlocked, he remembered, when he went downstairs to supper — there was little enough among his odds and ends of belongings that anyone would be apt to steal. The knob turned under his fingers, the panel swung back. But then Dan Temple halted in his tracks, powerless in the sudden grip of amazement.

She had been sitting on the edge of the bed and she rose quickly as he entered, faced him in the glow of the lamp she'd lighted. She was dressed simply, in white — a pure color that set off the auburn of her hair and the flawless beauty of her skin. The cut of the gown was artfully fashioned, molding to her body and accenting subtly the full roundness of her breast. She said, in a voice that trembled: "Dan —"

Slowly he came into the room, and closed the door; the weight of his shoulders against the panel clicked the catch into place and its sound was startlingly loud in the quiet.

Dan stayed that way a long moment, his eyes filled with the presence of Stella Ramsey, his mind stumbling before the question of what could have brought her to his room. He put the question into words, then — blunter and harsher than he intended them: "What are you doing here?" And added, in a flash of bitter insight, "Abel sent you, didn't he?"

Her hand was on the tarnished brass of the bedstead; it tightened there, and her head shook a little as she met his eyes. "Please don't judge him. You mustn't — not you, Dan. He isn't made of the same stuff as you; he can be broken. But I'm still his sister, and he means a great deal to me; and that's why I've come to — to plead for him!"

They faced each other in the dim light, with the dingy walls close about them and the cheap, ruined furnishings; and Temple said roughly, "It wasn't necessary. I'd already made up my mind, when I learned he'd run away rather than face me. He's not worth my trouble. Tell him, from me, that he can come out of hiding; I'm heading for my ranch, and I promise not to bother him."

"But I'm going to ask even more than this of you, Dan," she replied. "I want you to go back to work for us."

"No!" His head jerked, to the violence of his feeling. "After what's happened? How much would you ask a man to take?"

"Please, Dan!"

She came straight to him, and placed a hand upon his arm; it went right beneath her touch — perhaps with some dawning, inner consciousness in Dan Temple that his protests were vain, that she could and would talk him into anything she wanted.

"Believe me, I wouldn't ask it if there were any other way. But we need you, Dan! I don't know what will happen if you refuse to help us. They've already held up one of our stages. Because you were there, the money was returned and nothing lost. But next time — if you leave us now —"

"Maybe there won't be a next time." His voice was wooden, without conviction.

"There will be," she replied, quietly. "Someone is out to beat Great Western; you yourself gave us the first warning of it. Now it's known all over town that this stranger, this — Reed Lawler —" her red lips were touched with loathing as she spoke the name — "is setting up his new company, to give us competition. Don't you see the size of it? Let trouble hit at our stages a few times more, without you to ward it off; let John Evans lose a payroll shipment or two. What do you think then?"

He wasn't yet ready to surrender to her. "I'm not the only gunman you could hire," he said harshly, stubbornly. "The woods are full of them."

"But not men such as you — men we know we can depend on." She shook her head; lampglow found glints of golden light in the rich copper of her hair — and the glint of tears in her eyes. "It's to be a fight, Dan! And can you really imagine my brother standing up to a thing like that? As for me, I have no weapons; I'm only a woman —"

The irony of her words struck him with heavy force, as he felt his own defenses crumble before them. Struggling still, he knew already that he was lost.

"All right!" he cried half-angrily. "You can tell your brother to come out of hiding, and I'll go back to work for him!"

Even as he spoke the fateful words he was remembering his resolve of a moment before, and the free, high warmth that had been in him then. He was remembering too the image of the man whining and smirking over the dollar that had been thrown to him, and his mouth hardened at the thought. But it was not he who had done the begging, after all. There was at least that difference.

Then all thoughts were blotted from him as the girl's arms lifted and crept about his shoulders. Her lovely face near his, her breath against his cheek, she whispered, "Thank you, Dan Temple — thank you! You'll never regret it! I promise you won't!" And his own arms tightened about her compulsively, a little blindly. His mouth went down upon hers and felt the response of her kiss; in his hungry arms was the warmth and softness of her, and he thought almost he could feel the beating of her heart against his own.

He released her then, but she drew back without haste from his arms; for a moment her hand touched his cheek, lingeringly. "You're awfully nice, Dan!" she murmured.

"Even if I am a gunman and a tough?" something made him say harshly.

She smiled, and her red lips were teasing; he thought, half-mocking. But what she said was, "You shouldn't run yourself down!"

After that she moved to the door and he stood aside, opening it for her. Stella passed close to him, and paused with one hand raised against the jamb as she smiled back at him across her shoulder, to say good-night, the soft wealth of coppery tresses brushing her cheek. Even when she had left, the scent she wore remained with him, and every word and touch that had been ex-changed. He watched her down the cor-ridor, her slim white shape oddly contrasted with its drabness.

Only after Stella Ramsey had gone from sight did Dan Temple grow aware of the man who stood in front of a door across the hall, a key in the lock.

The man was staring at Temple, and the crossing of their glances was like a blow jarring him out of a trance. He turned back into the room, but he had taken only a step or two when something pulled him about and wrenching the door open again he strode out and across the hall. The man had his own door open now and was just moving across the threshold when Dan reached him and dropped a hand upon his shoulder. "A word with you, friend!" said Temple heavily.

The other turned a half-scared look on him. He was nobody Dan had ever seen before — a commercial traveler, judging from the plain stamp of his appearance. He started to stammer something but Temple cut him off.

"Look! This is none of your business — you understand that, don't you?"

"Why, sure!" the man showed the gleam of a gold front tooth as he grinned a little, nervously. "You were doing all right, partner. She had real class. Far be it from me to butt in." He winked, in an attempt at vulgar humor.

Dan Temple lifted one hand, balled into a fist; with the other he nailed his man, twisting a handful of coat and shirt-front and slamming him up against the edge of the door. "You'll keep your dirty mouth shut!" he growled. "Whatever you may have thought you saw, you were mistaken. Remember that! And you better not do any talking about it!"

He left that threat, and turning his back on the frightened drummer walked back into his room and slammed the door.

This aftermath had soured something of the moment with Stella; it completed what the tawdry surroundings had begun, in making the whole incident somehow sordid and unclean. The sense of her nearness, the memory of her kiss and the warmth of her in his arms, were already lost and gone. He knew only that he wanted no more of this place — not tonight, not after this.

Quickly, he set to work throwing his saddleroll together. The open night upon the trail, and then the lonely solitude of his homestead cabin, would be welcome to him now.

CHAPTER SIX

One day out of three, with the chores piling up and no telling when they would ever be done. . . .

From earliest dawn until close toward nightfall, Dan Temple labored on his place, putting up the wire Ruth Chess had brought out from town for him three nights ago.

Toward noon a sheet of gray cloud ceiling came pushing in across the sky, with a stiff wind behind it, and for a good two hours it rained — mean, needle-sharp, and miserable for a man at work with a posthole digger, his head bent and the icy water running down beneath the neck of his slicker and inside his sleeves. Later, the rain stopped and the clouds broke apart, and the wet earth steamed under a slanting April sun; and this was hardly an improvement.

But Dan Temple kept after it, doggedly, and it seemed to him when he knocked off at the end of the long day that he had accomplished two men's work. Tired as he was, his spirits lifted at this evidence of progress, and he was in a comparatively good mood as he cleaned up and saddled once more for the ride into Dragoon.

This mood suffered its first setback when, coming into the lamplit town, he turned toward the livery and passed an open-front shed that stood a few doors away from it. The shed had been abandoned and unused, in all the months of his familiarity with the town, except as a posting medium for circus broadsides and patent remedy advertisements; but tonight it was strangely alive with lantern light and the pungent odor of new paint, and looking in through the wide front opening as he passed Dan Temple was surprised to see that it now contained two big Concord coaches, standing side by side and gleaming a bright red and yellow and blue. The dirt floor of the shed was spotted with spilled paint, and two workmen were cleaning their brushes in turpentine as they prepared to knock off after the completion of their day's job. Dan could see that the coaches were not new, but after a final coat they would offer that impression. And he knew they were not Ramsey coaches.

He rode on, thoughtfully, and at the stable the old cripple who served as nightman greeted him with a nod and a confirming observation. "Something to roll agin' Great Western stock, hey? Looks like they're really after the Ramseys. And what'll your boss be doing about it?"

Temple answered briefly, "Go on giving the best service. Great Western has a reputation already built; it isn't easy to tear down a thing like that."

"Well, I dunno. Folks do say this Lawler has got a powerful lot of money in back of him. And supposin' they want to make a rate war of it?"

"Why, if it comes to that," said Dan, "I reckon we'll fight with the same weapons."

"I reckon so." The old man added, a

cryptic look stealing over his wrinkled face, "But that Stella girl, now — looks like she knows a way or two of her own of getting what she wants."

Dan turned on him sharply. "What did you say?" But the old man had already started hobbling away and Dan could only stare after him, wondering what in the world he could have meant and not liking the sound of it.

The old hostler was pretty plainly daft, however, and it was not worth pursuing the matter. Dan Temple left the stable and made for Rafferty's mercantile which he saw was still open to take care of a few late customers, and where he had a purchase to make. He turned up the steps fronting the lamp-bright building, and had almost reached the door when a girl came out of it, two men with her. Dan halted, seeing that it was Ruth Chess, and he spoke and touched his hat politely.

It halted her for just an instant; then, without any word at all, she averted her eyes and hurried past him. Dan Temple was astounded. He turned to call after her, but a voice in the doorway halted him, speaking his name sharply.

He turned back; Mark Chess and old Tom McNeil dropped down the steps. Their looks were dangerous with some unnamed anger, and as they halted just above him, where the lantern beside the door laid its circle of light squarely upon all their faces, Chess spoke again. "Leave Ruth alone, Temple. She doesn't want to talk to you."

You would not have called Mark Chess a tall man — that was not a family that ran to size — but he had a level eye like his daughter's, and an erectness of carriage that measured him well up alongside other men. He was elderly, Ruth having been born to him late in life. He had a fine shock of luxuriantly soft white hair, and his features were delicately molded; but there was strength and hardness to him for all that. His glance locked on Dan's as he made his sharp pronouncement.

Dan Temple could hardly believe what he had heard, except that the girl's strange behavior seemed clearly enough to confirm it. He shook his head, frowning and looking from one to another of the men before him. "I'm going to have to ask you to explain yourself, Mark," he said, finally.

The old puncher, Tom McNeil, cut in. "*You* answer one question, first, Temple," he rejoined. "Is it true you called your wolf off Abel Ramsey and agreed to go back to work for him — after you'd already promised to kill him on sight?"

"I'm working for him again — yes."

The old men exchanged glances. "I guess it's true enough, then," said Mark Chess.

"What is?" demanded Temple.

"That Stella Ramsey was seen coming out of your hotel room last night!"

Convulsively, Dan Temple's breath caught in his throat; his hands curled tight into fists. "So he talked, did he? The dirty little —" He caught himself, but the words were already spoken.

"Somebody's done some talking, apparently," agreed Chess. "The word is all over town. We're none of us blind, Temple — or fools, either. It must have taken quite a price to buy you back for Great Western, and make you renege on your threats against Abel Ramsey. And anyone older than a child could see what that price was."

Temple forced himself in check, then, until he could speak quietly. He said coldly, "Would it do any good if I were to tell you, whatever the appearances might be, your conclusions are as wrong as hell? If I told you that on my word of honor?"

Mark Chess was silent for a long moment. He gave his answer, then: "With a background like yours, Temple — I'm really not sure you have any honor! As for Stella

112

Ramsey —" His old shoulders lifted. "Naturally I don't like to condemn any woman, but we've always known she was wild. A cheap hustler for a daughter, and a weakling for a son — yes, I'm sorry for old Saul Ramsey, when I think of the legacy he left behind!"

"Saul Ramsey don't concern us," put in Tom McNeil doggedly; "especially as he's dead. But we gotta see that Ruth ain't bothered by this swell gent here. Damn you, Temple! I wish now I'd kept my nose out of your affairs and let them railroad you on that holdup charge!"

Surprise swamped for a moment the swirl of feelings in Dan Temple. He shot the old puncher a startled look. "You?" he echoed. "Was it you found the evidence to clear me?" He remembered, suddenly, how McNeil had been with Ramsey and the sheriff in the courthouse hallway yesterday morning when he was released; Dan remembered wondering, then, at his presence.

"If I did," replied the old man, tartly, "it was only because Ruth made me do it, and not because I expected any thanks — or wanted any, from the likes of you."

Mark Chess said quietly, "I guess it should be plain now where we all stand?"

"Plain enough!" Dan's words were clipped

and angry, his gray eyes smoldering. "Let me make it just this much plainer: it doesn't matter a hell of a lot what you think of me, but keep your dirty talk away from Stella Ramsey! Because, I'll smash any man I hear repeating such lies — and it won't save him because he happens to have gray in his beard!"

"You can't smash a whole town, Dan," said Chess. "I'm no talebearer, and except that Ruth was concerned I'd never have mentioned Stella's name, to you or anybody else. What's more, I'll never mention it again and Tom won't, either; we get no pleasure from spreading filth.

"But you are going to hear this talk, all around you; and I'm afraid you're going to find out there's some things fists or guns can't stop. Gossip, for one. Especially when it's gossip that most people figure deserves to be credited."

He added crisply, "Goodnight, Temple!" And on that note he nodded curtly and swung away from Dan, and Tom McNeil trailed him. Neither of the two old men looked back. Dan stood where he was, at the foot of the steps, staring after them with a welter of emotions boiling inside him.

He heeled around then and tramped up the broad planks and into the lamplit interior of the store. The familiar scents greeted him — of new leather, and kerosene, and molasses, and cloth goods lying in bolts on the long counters; and also of tobacco smoke issuing from half a dozen lighted cigarettes and corncob pipes. The usual loungers were there, munching crackers from the big barrel and exchanging idle joshing. At Dan's entrance this talk quieted oddly, and he saw all their eyes swing to rivet upon him.

With little more than a glance for any of them, Dan Temple strode back to give his order to the Irishman at the rear counter, and arrange that it be ready for him to pick up on his return from tomorrow's stage run. This business took a matter of ten minutes or so, and Dan noticed how the storekeeper conducted it with a scrupulous regard for formalities, and none of the familiar banter with which he normally treated a regular customer. The man was in fact highly ill at ease, and making a painful effort not to show it.

Dan swung about suddenly, ran a sharp look over the half dozen faces under the oil lamp. He surprised a ludicrous medley of expressions, and more than one mocking grin that faded quickly before his stare and left its owner loose-lipped and blank of eye.

115

Dan felt the muscles of his right arm draw up, and then he remembered what Mark Chess had told him: *You can't smash a whole town. . . . There's some things fists or guns can't stop!"*

"I'll be around for that stuff in a couple of days," he grunted shortly. "Have it ready." And he walked out of the store, his face stiffly expressionless.

As chance would have it, at that moment a quick tapping of heels sounded along the hard-surfaced pathway and he saw Stella Ramsey coming toward him, alone. Dan Temple wanted to draw back and avoid a meeting; but he was not small-spirited enough for that. He knew he would have to face her eventually and she had more than likely already seen him, anyway, there in the light from the mercantile doorway.

So he waited, and as she came even with him, he saw the whiteness of the face she lifted. She said, in a level voice, "Good evening, Dan."

He nodded, his words carefully formal. "How are you, Stella?"

"Well enough." She nodded ahead along the street. "I was just going home. Will you walk along with me? I think my brother wants to talk to you about the run tomorrow."

Dan hesitated. "I could drop by later on —"

"No," she said, and her voice held a note of defiance. "I want you to walk with me, Dan."

He knew for sure then that she had heard the talk, and that this was her proud way of answering it. He nodded and came down to her; at once her hand was at his elbow. And like that they started along the path, through the banded light and shadow, Stella's full skirt whispering against the rough denim of his pantleg and their footsteps making an odd duet of sound.

He tilted a glance at the top of the auburn hair so close beside his shoulder, saw how erectly she carried it, and how her own shoulders were set and proud beneath the scarf she wore against the evening's chill. Something went out to her from him, a swelling of admiration for her calm strength and for the way she was standing up to the hostility of the town.

"Stella —"

"It's all right, Dan." Her fingers tightened the crook of his arm. "Why talk about it? Why give it the — the dignity of caring what they say?"

"But we can't let it go on!" he cried hoarsely. "For myself, it doesn't matter —

117

such talk does nothing to a man. But, you!"

"What do I care what's on their nasty tongues and in their nasty minds?" she retorted. "If we rise to their baiting, they'll never let us alone; but if we don't give them any satisfaction they'll tire of the game fast enough. You watch and see! I know these neighbors of mine — what cheap, small-minded creatures they can be!"

There was such bitterness in her words that Dan heard her, aghast. He had considered himself a cynical person but to hear such things from Stella disquieted him. "You hate this town, don't you?" he exclaimed, suddenly.

Her shoulders lifted, settled in a hopeless shrug. "I was born in St. Louis, Dan," she said. "I was eight years old when my father brought us out here — just old enough to have seen the difference between that world and this. And old enough to see how my mother stifled here and died, longing for the life she'd given up to follow Saul Ramsey. I loved my mother, Dan; I'm very like her. And I'm not going to waste out my life here — or let cheap, small-town gossip poison me! It isn't that important. It's — it's not worth noticing!"

Dan Temple walked beside her in silence for a while, considering what she had told him. It was a side of her that had never been shown him before; he thought all at once that he understood her better — understood the tormented drives that must work at cross-purposes within her, holding her to the task of saving Great Western and, through it, her weakling brother; while all the time — with her whole soul and body — she detested the fate that life had shoved upon her.

She went on now, her voice altered, the fierceness gone from it: "You're the only person I've ever talked to of this, Dan Temple — the only one I've felt would understand. Because — you're not a part of this town yourself, you don't belong to it any more than I. You've been across the horizons. You know how far life in a place like this falls short of what it might be."

He began to say, "I've sort of liked it here, myself," but with the words on his tongue he hesitated and then let them go unspoken. He wondered in that moment if perhaps Stella was right. He tried, as they walked together through the silent street, to look back across the entire span of months here and decide if it had really been worth the labor and sacrifice it cost him — whether the satisfactions had been compensation for the narrowing of his horizons to this one small segment of the earth. But it was too big a question to be settled, all in a moment; and now all such thoughts were broken off as the bulky shape of a man stepped out of a doorway, nearly colliding with them, and quickly drew back with a murmur of apology.

It was Reed Lawler; the yellow-haired man recognized Dan and his companion at the same instant. Faintly, Dan could see the virile, good-looking face of the man and the twisted smile that began to quirk his lips. He saw Lawler's slow glance run from his own face to that of Stella Ramsey; the lopsided smile cut deeper. But there was no warmth in the shadowed eyes.

"Well, well," murmured the big man. It was his tone rather than what he said that gave the words an inflection of sardonic amusement and that set Dan's blood to boiling a little.

"You wanted something, Lawler?" he demanded, and was angry with himself that it came out so harshly.

"Oh, no! No!" was the quick, offhand reply. "I wouldn't think of interrupting!" He drew back, nodding and lifting his hat to the girl. He had been freshly shaved and barbered, and Dan caught the odor of bay rum on him. It seemed suddenly a very distasteful smell.

Stella Ramsey was observing carefully something on the other side of the street and refusing even to look at the blond man. Grimly, Dan took her arm. He said, "That's damned kind of you, Lawler!" And with no other word steered the girl past the other man.

Reed Lawler faded back against the building front, making room for them; Temple knew the sardonic eyes were on them as they went away from him along the pathway.

At his side, Stella Ramsey's slim body held a stiffness that was communicated to Dan through the smooth flesh of the arm beneath his hand. She said, suddenly, when they were beyond earshot: "The others, I can stand. But from him —"

He halted abruptly, turning to face her. "Wait a minute! Is it Reed Lawler that's been spreading this talk? If I was sure of it —"

"How can we be sure?" She shook her head helplessly. "But who else would be deliberately keeping it alive? Who else would pick this cheap way to smear the Ramsey name? That smug, nasty —"

Dan took her arm again. He wanted to change the subject; it seemed to him she was letting herself become more worked up than the thing deserved. He said, "We'll forget it. As you say, people have short memories. This talk will die. If Lawler wants to wreck Great Western it will have to be out on the stage trails — not with slanderous whispers. . . ."

But he was less than completely convinced of this himself, as he went with her up a dark street toward the ugly, gingerbread-encrusted mammoth of a house that stood behind its picket railings at the edge of town — the gone-to-seed mansion of old Saul Ramsey, left as part of a dubious legacy to his children.

They walked up the weed-grown and neglected flagstone path to the deep veranda, where light showed behind the heavy drapes of the living room window. The door was locked and Stella had forgotten her key, so Dan pulled the bell cord for her and they stood waiting, oddly constrained and silent now, and stared at the picture of a stag, a mosaic of colored glass, that filled the door window. Then a shadow fell across the glass; the latch lifted, and Abel Ramsey opened to them.

When his glance hit Dan Temple he stiffened, visibly, and his sullen face took on a slight color. It was the first time they had met, face to face, since that scene yesterday in the courthouse. Dan made no move to ease the awkward moment, but got a certain hard pleasure in holding the silence until Ramsey wavered and broke gaze before his own gray stare.

Abel Ramsey stepped back, then, pulling the door wider and not looking at either of them directly. He mumbled, "It's a good thing you've showed up. John Evans is here."

"Evans?" his sister echoed, and as Ramsey jerked his head toward the living room archway she hurried past him. Temple followed, pausing to drop his dusty Stetson on a table in the hall. Behind him, Ramsey closed the heavy door.

The living room was narrow and long, filled with the massive furniture of an earlier day that must have cost old Saul Ramsey a handsome sum to freight this far west. It was ugly enough in spite of certain obvious attempts on Stella's part to modernize it. A small pine-knot fire was crackling in the black maw of the huge fireplace, and before the marble mantelpiece John Evans stood warming his backside as he nodded to the greeting of the girl.

Temple hardly considered the night chilly enough to warrant a fire; but this room was one that needed some cheering note of warmth to combat the oppressive weight of its furnishings. And John Evans had always struck him as a hopelessly thin-blooded individual. Probably wore red flannels under his pin-striped cutaway and tight trousers and shed them only on the first of May.

Stella had removed her shawl and dropped it across the back of an overstuffed chair. Her white shoulders were creamy in the lamplight, against the rich auburn of her hair. She said, in a business voice, "What's the trouble, Mr. Evans?"

The syndicate man made an uncomfortable, writhing gesture with his shoulders. "No trouble," he assured her hastily. "At least, I — I hope not. I didn't like coming here this way, but — Well, after Mr. Lawler saw me and I had been thinking over what he said —"

"What's Reed Lawler got to do with it?" Stella Ramsey demanded, with sharp apprehension.

Her brother had entered the room behind Dan Temple; it was he that answered her, angrily: "He's trying to get the Syndicate account away from us, is all. He's trying to outbid us."

Dan Temple, observing all this in silence, thought: So it's starting this early!

"I haven't made him any promises, you understand," Evans put in quickly. "I

124

haven't, and I don't want to. I know it would be a very serious thing for Great Western, and naturally I'd be reluctant to make such a switch except on the most careful consideration. Especially as Great Western has given me very satisfactory service — up till very recently," he qualified.

"What do you mean, 'up to recently'?" snapped Dan Temple, cutting in. "What have you had to complain about? You lost one shipment, yes — but you got it back again. That's still a perfect record, by my way of looking at it!"

Evans made that writhing motion again. "Yes, of course. Nevertheless," he pointed out, "you'll have to agree that there was an uncomfortable — delay!" He cleared his throat, a sharp sound in the stuffy room. Stella Ramsey threw Dan a glance that eloquently asked him not to interfere, and turned back to the syndicate man.

"Just what kind of a proposition is Reed Lawler trying to sell you?"

"Well, it's like this. He came to my office this afternoon and told me of his plans for establishing a stage and freight line into the mountains, rivaling yours. Of course, none of it was news to me — been a matter of general knowledge hereabouts, for days now, especially as we've all seen the coaches

125

he's brought in, and the wagon yard he's putting up. I started to tell the man that in my opinion he was throwing away good money, bucking a company as long established and well-thought-of as Great Western; but then he said something that — well, I'll admit it set me to wondering a little."

"Let's have it!" snapped Stella Ramsey.

She hadn't moved, or taken her eyes from Evans' face; her steady regard seemed to turn him uneasy. He edged away from the fireplace, and Dan Temple couldn't be sure that the sheen of sweat he saw on the man's sallow features was put there entirely by the warmth of the pine-knot fire.

He found himself thinking: What does the gent use for a spine? Certainly it's his privilege to hand his company's freighting business to any outfit that will give the best service — he doesn't have to stand for this grilling. . . . At the same time it struck Dan that Stella Ramsey knew exactly what she was doing, and how to handle this man. Almost like a school teacher with a guilty child — and John Evans was taking it.

The syndicate man dragged out a handkerchief and ran it around his neck, digging under the tight collar with it. "Lawler claims there's no certainty that what happened to one of your coaches couldn't happen again.

With all respect to Temple here —" Evans jerked a quick nod in his direction — "he's only one man, after all — and the only one your organization employs who is handy with a gun. Lawler says there's no reason to believe the crooks will lay off my payroll shipments because of any single individual. The next time, he says, they'll merely make it a point to knock off the shotgun guard, first thing, with an ambush bullet — and then do whatever they like with the stage and the strongbox."

"Oh! He says that, does he?" grunted Dan Temple, and his jaw tightened.

"But if I switch to his company," Evans went on, speaking hurriedly, "he guarantees there'll be no such trouble. Because, Lawler will hire a guard of outriders to protect the stage, every mile of the road between here and the mine. Twenty men, if he thinks it will take that many to keep the road agents from tackling it —"

"Twenty men!" Stella Ramsey's eyes flashed scorn. "Twenty outriders, at gun-men's wages! And who do you suppose is going to pay those wages, John Evans? Had you thought of that? Great Western has always believed in fair rates, even when we could have pushed them sky high and got them because we were the only company operating; and I think you know it! But let this — this Reed Lawler —" the name seemed to taste bad as she spoke it — "take our business away from us and crowd us out, and then how much do you think it's going to cost you to supply your payrolls with a twenty-man escort? Tell me — just how much?"

In the face of her outburst, the syndicate man could only shake his head nervously, stammering for words. He managed to get out: "Please! Remember, I haven't accepted his offer. But — it *is* a guarantee —"

Dan Temple cut in then: "If that's all you want, here's a guarantee for you, Evans: I'll give you my personal assurance that the next payroll shipment gets through unmolested. And I won't need any twenty men to do it!"

CHAPTER SEVEN

All their eyes were on him now, startled and questioning. Abel Ramsey exclaimed, "That's a lot for you to take on yourself, Temple!"

"Well, there's the offer," he answered, indifferently. "It happens I've got my personal reasons for not liking this Lawler gent, and for wanting to see him stopped."

"But how, Dan?" the girl demanded. "We've got to know, before we'll allow you to take any such risk as this!"

"No risk to it, as long as it's possible to keep a secret. . . . How soon do you want a payroll shipment sent through, Evans?"

The syndicate man said, "Tomorrow. The one that was taken from the stage three days ago hasn't gone up yet. The men at the mine are still waiting to be paid off."

"All right. Tomorrow, then — but not on the stage. The weekly supply wagon pulls out of here in the afternoon. Without anyone knowing, we'll load the money in with the rest of the stuff and send it up that way. And no guard, you understand! I'll ride the stage in the morning, as usual — but carrying an empty strongbox in the boot." His mouth quirked, in a humorless smile. "You see, that's all the plan I have — just the old shell trick, figuring that anyone looking for the pea will lift the wrong shell!"

He settled back then, against the edge of a heavy mahogany table, and folded his arms as he watched his idea take foot in their minds. He saw Abel Ramsey's knobby forehead puckered in a frown, his hollow cheeks indrawn as he considered. He saw Stella's wide look, and the way her lower lip caught between white teeth. Then he swung his glance toward John Evans, as the syndicate man drew himself up, letting the wind trail through pursed lips before he spoke the first word.

"It might work," Evans said slowly. "It's just simple enough that it might. Though I do think there ought to be some kind of a guard —"

"No guard!" repeated Dan, flatly. "It would give us dead away. If I hear that you've tried slipping a man into that supply wagon, I take back my guarantee!"

It was Stella who saw a fault in the scheme. "Dan, I don't like it!" she exclaimed. "What it amounts to is you setting yourself for a clay pigeon, just asking someone to put a bullet in you!"

"That," said Temple, without emotion, "is what I'm paid for. It's the chance I take. But even if it happens — they still won't get anything for their trouble but an empty express box!"

Abel Ramsey looked at the syndicate man. He said, "Well, what about it, Evans? Do you want to try this? Or will it be Reed Lawler's army?"

In indecision, Evans ran a palm slowly across his mouth. "With the people I work for," he said finally, "you make one mistake and you're out." Then he added, his head lifting, "But they have little use, either, for a man who won't take a chance. . . . All right, Ramsey. We'll try it this way."

"Good!" A decision made, a program charted, Abel Ramsey could function adequately; it was in forcing the decision — making up his own or another man's mind — that he suffered his doubts and anguished insecurities. He said now, excitedly, "I'll give Becker his orders, first thing in the morning."

A moment later, the little group broke up. Dan Temple was first to leave. He got his hat from the hall table and already had the door open when Stella came after him, calling his name. Her face, lifted to his, held a look that sent a tingling warmth through him.

She told him, "Nobody remembered to say, 'Thank you,' Dan. But I think you know how I — how we feel."

"Forget it. My reasons were personal ones. You don't have to thank me."

"But there's one thing." And she hesitated; it seemed to him the only time he had ever caught her in any sign of uncertainty. He wondered what she meant to tell him.

"I'm sorry, Dan," she said then, "you had to watch my performance, tonight, with John Evans. I'm not that kind of a person,

honestly; but — Well, one of the Ramseys
has got to be strong. And you see what Abel
is. He hardly opened his mouth; he was glad
enough to let me do the talking. And a man
like Evans can be handled in only one way."

That she felt a need to make such an
explanation at all was the only thing that
mattered to Dan Temple — that, and the
fact that his opinion meant so much to her.
He said, a little gruffly, "I figured it was that
way. You didn't have to explain, Stella."

"Thank you." She showed him her smile,
slow and secret. It happened to be at that
instant that John Evans came into the hall
archway.

As he saw the pair of them, close together,
he hauled up short and a ludicrous expression crossed his face. The girl drew back,
without haste. Dan glanced at the other
man, and smiling thinly he pulled the door
wide.

"After you, sir!"

Evans made an embarrassed noise in his
throat that wasn't quite coherent enough to
be speech, and clapping on his hat he
ducked out between them, his shoulders
hunched and eyes averted. Listening to his
quick footsteps cross the veranda and hurry
off along the flagstoned walk, Dan Temple
observed drily, "I'm afraid we embarrassed

him. He's heard the talk too, apparently."

Then he looked and saw that her mouth was drawn tight, her eyes glinting. She said abruptly, "There's to be a dance Wednesday night. I want you to take me!"

He started. "You real sure of that?"

"Don't you want to?" she countered.

"Certainly. But wouldn't it be — ?"

"Throwing the thing in their faces? That's just what I intend! It's the only way to stop the talking — by showing it doesn't make any difference to us, and going them one better."

He hesitated for a long moment, considering the line of argument. Then he nodded, slowly, and touched her shoulder. "Wednesday night," he repeated.

He left quickly. She was still in the open door, a slim shadow, still watching him as he turned away through the gate in the pickets and went down the dark street toward the heart of town.

More clouds came with morning, and a chill wind that blew the gritty dust about the town, that lifted blinding, stinging clouds of it against the horses stamping fitfully in the stage traces. Dan Temple, lounging in his place on the high seat, squinted against this dusty blast and sheltered his cigarette behind a cupped palm as he waited, shotgun across his knees.

The wind had its way, too, with John Evans and the clerk, Becker, as they came along the path from the syndicate office, bringing the express box according to the usual morning routine. It lifted Evans' coat-tails and had him clinging to his hat with one hand to clamp it in place, his face screwed up ludicrously. He was letting Becker carry the box, alone; and Dan scowled as he saw this. When they reached the coach and he leaned to take the box from Becker's hands, he grunted, "You could at least try to pretend it isn't empty, couldn't you? Want to give the show away before we're even started?"

Paul Becker met his look with black, sullen eyes that held nothing. There was something about this man that always seemed to rouse in Dan an unadmirable impulse to prod him, to try to break through the man's cold reserve — but never with any clear success. Even now, when he'd been caught in an error, he showed no indication that Temple's sharp speech had any effect other than to heighten for an instant the remote, contemptuous hostility that always colored the few moments of contact between them.

He turned away then, and Dan lifted the

empty box and stowed it into the boot beneath him. For just a moment he found himself checking over this plan of his, searching it for flaws with an uncomfortable awareness of risk. An image of Vern Jackman's gaunt and bearded face and crafty eyes flashed before his vision. He thought suddenly: Vern knows me too well; he was always cleverer than I, and he savvies how my mind works. . . . But such speculations were futile and he pushed them away; and then Sim Pearson was climbing up to take the reins, and it was too late to call a halt or change the program, even had he wanted to. He shut his mind to vague forebodings, then, and settled back upon the hard cushions bracing himself for the jolt of Pearson's explosive start.

The horses leaped into the collars; with earsplitting yells and a popping of the long whip, they were off. The town blurred past beyond a screen of scouring dust. As the last of the buildings fell behind and Sim Pearson settled back to the monotony of the run, he shot a sideward look at Dan Temple, gave him a brief nod and then slid his glance quickly back to the rumps of the running horses again. Sim was ill at ease, and understandably. It was his first contact with Temple since the day of the holdup;

and after the trouble he had caused Dan over that, he could hardly know what to expect now from the dark and silent man beside him.

Dan let him stew, his cool glance watching the unwinding ribbon of road. Heavy, angry clouds weighted down the sky above timbered ridges, distantly ahead. Dan had a poncho in the boot, should rain hit them; meanwhile it was pleasant to be rid of the hot sun. There were no passengers. Outwardly, at least, this had the appearance of an ordinary, routine run, on schedule, through the pass to Antelope.

Then, a short mile or two out of Dragoon, Dan saw the mounted man in the road ahead and he straightened a little, frowning. The rider lifted an arm, waved it once and let it fall again; otherwise he made no movement as the heavy coach bore down on him.

Pearson was the first to recognize the sheriff. 'Gentry!' he grunted. "Now, what do you suppose he wants!" And prepared to set his foot upon the brake.

As the coach rocked to a halt and the dust swept away, the sheriff kneed his horse over beside the front wheel. He nodded to the driver and the guard. "I'm going along, this trip," he announced briefly. "Thought I'd wait, though, until you got clear of town."

136

He jerked his head toward the coach. "No one inside?"

"No," said Pearson.

"Hold it up a minute, then, and I'll just pile in there."

It was a livery horse the sheriff was riding — one that would return to its barn when he set it loose. He dismounted, tied up the reins and gave the animal's dusty flank a swat to start it heading back toward town. Then he climbed into the coach, grunting a little as he hauled his heavy weight up the iron step. Sim Pearson gave the sheriff barely time to settle before he had his teams in motion again.

Dan Temple had said nothing; his reaction to this development was not entirely unmixed. The sheriff's capable gun would be considerable help in case the coach should run into trouble. But he had wanted Vern Jackman to himself, without the law interfering. It was too personal a matter for that.

They rolled on through the gray, gusty morning, through a land that was drab and without color under the lowering sky. Contrary to the usual lethargic boredom the trip engendered in him, today there was a tension in Dan Temple that centered somewhere vaguely in the vicinity of his shoulder muscles. From time to time he shifted position, twisting his shoulders inside the leather jacket to try and work this unnatural stiffness out of them before it knotted into something painful. He tried to build another cigarette but gave it up and tossed the paper and tobacco away when the sharp, beating wind foiled his attempt. He settled back, instead, forcing a looseness into his long body. And now the ground began to lift and the first pines, their green needles looking leathery and black in the lightless day, fell back behind them.

Climbing, they came nearer to the clouds. The upper peaks were lost behind misty, shifting streamers of fog, and the thickening ranks of spruce and cedar held the damp breath of the day in their branches. As the stage road leveled out upon the scattered cedar bench, a fine rain began needling out of the overcast. Dan fished his poncho out from the boot and pulled it on; Sim Pearson merely hunched deeper into the collar of his windbreaker, scowling into the peppering rain.

And now they were lifting into the yellow pine, and the vague tension Dan had known took on sharper meaning. He paid a close attention on the crowding ranks of the timber now, finding there numberless excellent places where a man could rest his rifle barrel against a straight-boled pine and pick his shot, carefully, on a man on the approaching stage box. Get the guard first, and the rest would be easy. . . . Reed Lawler had said that, and that was undoubtedly the way it would come. Vern Jackman, his gaunt, bearded cheek pressed to the rifle's stock, his glassy eye perhaps even now narrowing on the target. . . .

Just ahead loomed the granite-walled gap toward the higher passes. And as Sim Pearson began to gather the ribbons and ready his foot on the brake for his customary halting of the laboring teams, Dan Temple quietly lifted the sixgun from holster and held it in his lap, knowing that this would be a critical moment. But his quick glance, scanning the timber, saw no movement there. The stage dragged to a halt. Pearson stretched cramped limbs, stepped down the wheel for a look at the off-leader's harness, which wasn't buckled to suit him. Still there was nothing — no sound except for the blowing of the horses and the scream of a camp-robber that started and faded out, back in the fastnesses of the forested hills. The trees stood about, heavy with fog and drizzling rain.

Sheriff Gentry had opened the coach door and was out stumping around to stretch himself. He came over to where Temple sat and, leaning a shoulder against the wheel, cocked an eye up at the other man as he fumbled a cigar out of a pocket and bit off the end. "Quite enough so far," the sheriff rumbled. He added, "And miserable!" He shivered and pulled his coat tighter about him.

Dan said nothing, his eyes on the silent surrounding timber and the rocky gap ahead. A conviction was dawning on him that it would be like this the rest of the way in; that nothing would happen. That his precautions had been needless, and Vern Jackman had no designs this time on the Yellow Jack shipments.

Or maybe —

Another possibility struck him, like a blow. No, he told himself. It was out of the question; surely Great Western's enemies couldn't have been so knowing, so far ahead of him in his effort to ward them off. Yet all at once he was figuring the distances to Antelope and to Dragoon, and as Sim Pearson came back to his place on the seat Dan said, "Let's get moving! Make the best time you can, fellow. I've got a hunch and I don't like it!"

The driver shot him a look but decided against asking questions. "All right," he grunted. "I'll do what I can; but remember — these are only hosses. I ain't going to run them to death just on the strength of another man's hunch!" Still, he had the teams strung out at a good pace as they left there and started up into the pass.

Scattered through these hills were the ruins of twenty camps like Antelope that had seen their day and vanished when the mineral that gave them life pinched out and the mines closed down. Antelope, no more promising than any of the others when it began its fevered life, still hung on, still producing mineral; frame buildings, hugging crooked and narrow streets that wound across the mountain slope, and surrounded by the ugly tailings and the black mine shafts and the hacked-out timber that generally marked such places.

The stage from Dragoon came rocking in at the end of a record run, and amid the usual excitement attending this twice-weekly break in the dead monotony of life here. At the log station Dan Temple was already coming down from his perch before the iron brakeshoe had quite taken hold on rim-iron. As he started to turn away an anxious bespectacled man in a business suit confronted him — an underling from the

Yellow Jack, who had been waiting with a pair of armed guards for the stage to appear.

"Well, where's the payroll?" this one wanted to know. He added quickly, on a note of alarm. "Don't tell me —"

"No, it isn't stolen," said Temple, chafing at the delay. "Not this time; we didn't bring it. You'll have to wait till later for explanations, though — I got a ride to make!"

He broke free, leaving the clerk standing there; a moment later he collared the station boss and said, "Get me one of your broncs. A fast one."

"Make that two," rumbled the sheriff's voice. Tyler Gentry met Temple's quick glance. "I'll just ride along with you, Temple. Trouble seems to hit where you are."

Dan started to tell him to mind his own business, but held his tongue. The hills were free and he couldn't stop the lawman from riding wherever he wanted in them. Shrugging, he turned away impatiently. Would they never get those horses up?

But at last the mounts were saddled, ready, and Dan took the stirrup and went into leather. His borrowed horse was a gray, with plenty of bottom and the long, speedy build of a racer — Great Western kept good animal stock. Not even looking to see if the sheriff was ready, Dan Temple pushed through the crowd at the station and headed down the steep-pitched and muddy street. But almost at once Gentry had caught up with him, his own white-stockinged roan gelding kicking up gouts of black mud as he pulled it out of a near-stumble alongside Temple. The sheriff grunted, "In that big a hurry? Run a bronc into the ground at this rate!"

Dan said nothing. Nevertheless he checked his own impatience, and reined the bay in a little. After all, there was considerable distance to cover.

As they dropped away from the ugly mining town and lost it behind them in the first ranks of the timber, he computed the likely speed of the upcoming freight rig. Considering the time at which it would leave Dragoon, and the distances, they would be doing well to meet it much before it crossed the divide. He would have to discipline his patience, and settle to the ride that lay ahead of him.

After a bit the sheriff said, "You gonna tell me what this is all about, fellow? And where the hell it is we're riding in such a hurry?"

Scowling, looking straight ahead of him, Dan Temple answered curtly, "You'll find out when I do!" He wasn't in a mood for talk.

The rain had stopped, though scudding clouds still scoured the lower heavens. Temple had left his poncho in the boot of the stage, as well as the shotgun. There was no scabbard on the sheriff's saddle and Tyler Gentry had fastened the rifle to his saddle strings. Riding light, they made good time through the timber, steady drum of shod hoofs on wheel-packed stage road making the only alien sound in the solitude of the wind-swept forest. And it seemed to Dan that time stood motionless, in the dull half-gloom of the pines and the cloud wrack that obscured the westering sun.

When they began to climb toward the high point of the divide, where timber thinned out and became stunted and windbent with altitude, Dan Temple started hunting ahead for a first sign of the supply rig. As near as he could judge it should have covered this much distance in the time since its scheduled departure, down below. But the long moments passed; they came up into the pass itself and pulled in behind the shelter of a twisted cedar clump to let their borrowed horses blow, and still were without any sight or sound of the Ramsey wagon though now a considerable sweep of the eastern slopes lay open before them. Dan Temple looked down on that black mantling of timber, partly obscured by cloud streamers that drifted between. He was conscious of the lawman beside him; Tyler Gentry laid his own regard across those lower ranges and then let his look swing over to Temple's face. The weight of it was disturbing. He said, "Well?"

Still Temple said nothing. Turning to his horse, he pulled up the cinches and swung again to saddle. The two men went down out of the pass, over the steeper pitch of the switchback road, and the trees rose to encompass them.

A definite premonition of disaster had settled on Dan — a conviction, almost. There could of course be other reasons for their not having met the supply wagon to Antelope — a breakdown on the road, a lame horse, a delay in starting. But Temple's certainty was an irrational one that discounted all such explanations his reason could contrive.

He merely knew, now, what they were going to find around one of the turns in this timber-choked road; and as a result he felt almost no emotion when at last he got the first glimpse, and knew that what he had dreaded was a fact.

The wagon stood at an odd angle, pulled sharply over to the edge of the road. A smell of charred timbers tanged the air, growing quickly stronger as the riders spurted forward. After that they were reining down their horses, quieting the animals as they tried to shy. For there was blood there, too. The horses didn't like it, but a firm hand curbed them and for a long minute the men looked over the scene. You could read, plainly, what must have happened.

One of the lead team was down, dropped by a neatly placed bullet; dashes of a knife blade had set the rest loose, to scatter, leaving only the cut ends of the harness. The wagon had been fired but not successfully. The canvas had gone quickly, hanging on its steel bows, but the solidly built wagon-box was only partially consumed. One corner showed bad scorching but for the most part it had not burned.

Tyler Gentry shifted heavily in the saddle, "Where's the driver?" he muttered.

"There," said Dan, and pointed.

Booted legs projected past the far side of the rig, down in the dust, motionless. The two men dismounted and led their horses around that way, to look at the lifeless shape of the man, face down beside the wagon. He was one they had both known — a

146

Ramsey teamster named Ed Stacey. The sheriff leaned and turned him over, and that way they could see the blood in the dust, and soaked into the front of his flannel shirt. A chest wound, instantly fatal.

A gun lay not far from the dead hand and Gentry picked this up and showed the spent shell beneath the hammer, sniffed gingerly at the sour fouling of the barrel. He said, "Stacey was a stubborn fool — always. He tried a play and got it, dead center. If he'd held his hand maybe nothing would have happened to him."

Dan turned away and, stepping up the rear wheel hub, swung for a look into the body of the wagon that was still hot to the touch. Things there were a mess of burned and tumbled boxes, bags, other freight. It had been plowed through, efficiently, by someone who knew exactly what he was hunting for; and Dan Temple knew there was small point in looking for the Yellow Jack payroll in its metal box. It would not be there.

He swung down, cleaning black soot from his hands upon the thighs of his jeans. He met the sheriff's inquiring stare.

Temple made a sour face. "Well, you've guessed it, haven't you? The money was in the wagon — the stage carried an empty box."

"The hell you say! And whose fine scheme was that?"

"Mine!"

He waited for the sheriff's outburst; but Gentry only moved away a pace, and back again, his iron-gray head bent, his mouth thin and tight. "One man did this," he said, finally. "The tracks are plain. Just one man — and he's made fools of all of us! There'll be hell to pay, Temple!"

"They didn't need to send more than one," Temple's voice was bleak. "It was set up for them, that way, with no one but Ed Stacey to give them any trouble!"

The sheriff lifted chunky shoulders, settled them within his canvas windbreaker.

"Well, nothing more we can do here. The Ramseys will have to send up to salvage whatever they can. Give me a hand and we'll load Stacey into the wagon, for the time being, and then do some scouting. The sign should be less than two hours old, though it'll be hard to follow in this cross-grained country."

Stacey's body was still faintly warm, and not yet wholly stiff with death. He weighed little and they got him into the wagon easily enough and covered him with a tarp they dug out of the jumbled freight. Again in the saddle, Dan looked across at the older man who was slower to locate the stirrup and lift himself into leather.

He said, "So long, Sheriff. This time, I'm riding alone."

It got him a stabbing look. "Just what do you mean?" Gentry demanded. "Damn it, Temple! You're into this pretty deep; I don't like you running out on me, just when I need help cleaning up the mess you made!"

"When I'm wearing a deputy's badge," Dan retorted coldly, "I'll take your orders. Until then, I ride where and when I've a mind to! And I got business elsewhere!"

On that remark he jogged his pony and was gone before the sheriff could answer. He didn't doubt that he would hear about this later; and he knew Tyler Gentry could be a dangerous one to cross. But he had a purpose in riding now and he pushed on with it, a seething anger flaring in him now as his thoughts ran ahead.

When he had covered a mile, or a fraction under, along the town trail and had left the sheriff safely beyond sight, he quit the stage road abruptly and struck into the timber, threading a way among the close-growing, silver-gray trunks, working higher. Cold wetness hung in the needles of the pines, made the carpeted ground underfoot spongy and slick. Dan Temple kept a direct course.

He hardly noticed any more the chill that, cutting through his warm clothing, often put a shiver running through him.

Once, some ingrained training spoke a warning to him and he halted, drawing into a screen of jack pine while his mount rested and he made a sweeping, careful survey of the country below and behind him. Whatever had prompted the thought that there might be someone on his trail, he decided he was mistaken. He sent the gray forward again; and, in the last weakening light of a waning afternoon, came once again upon the abandoned mine with its slag heaps and gaping shafts, its decayed and crumbling buildings.

From the shelter of the aspens he looked down on this and found it utterly deserted. No smoke, no candle burning behind the dingy window, no movement. Dan kneed his horse forward, finally, and rode down across the weeds and the broken, rattling stone of the slope; he dropped the reins, and after a moment dismounted. There could be no mistake. This place had the ghostly, eerie silence of utter desertion. He was alone here.

He walked over to the main building, kicked open the squealing door. The room was empty. Nevertheless he strode inside, stood in the bleak half-darkness looking about at broken furnishings, the empty bunk and rusted stove without a chimney. That was when he noticed the paper, folded and propped upon the table top.

Taking it to the window, he opened it and found writing, penciled in a strongly masculine hand. It was a letter, addressed to himself. He read the message twice through, and as he did so the image of a narrow face, with its spade beard and mocking smile and agate eyes, came between him and the paper:

Danny,

I figured you would show up. Sorry I couldn't be around this time so we could talk over the old days some more, but naturally I can't afford the risk.

Don't feel too bad about today's doings, Danny. It was a pretty fair scheme, coming from you, and except for a tipoff you might have fooled us. But you've just made the job easier and I only hope the guy on the wagon doesn't play the fool and try to give me trouble.

Don't waste your time looking for me any longer. I've got a better hideout now — one even you aren't apt to find.

V.

Chagrin had its way with Temple; his fingers tightened, crushing the scrawled note into a ball, and he threw it from him. Still, in a way, he was almost relieved not to face the showdown with Vern Jackman. If Jackman had been here when he came, there would have to have been gunplay. Dan thought he could have won such a duel; but that wasn't the point.

He and Vern had taken different routes, but there were many memories yet to hold them together in spite of the thing that Jackman was doing to him now. It seemed inevitable, the way things were going, that the two of them would meet across gunsights before this ended; but he still did not like to think about it.

So it was with a draining sense of a crisis avoided that he turned again to leave that place. At the last moment he thought of the note and went back for it, retrieving it from behind the stove where it had fallen and shoving it into a pocket. Outside, he went into saddle; and his face was bleak now as he looked ahead to the reception that awaited him with the Ramseys in Dragoon.

There was something else, though — a single phrase in Jackman's note, echoing and re-echoing in his thoughts. It opened startling vistas that he needed time to think over and to work out exactly what obscure meaning they held for him. Those few words might be the key to unlock this entire, confusing mess. . . .

Not five minutes after the sounds of Temple's mount were muffled and lost, and empty silence once more settled over the abandoned mine workings, another rider melted out of the aspens and picked his way carefully down the uneven slope toward the ruined buildings. Sheriff Gentry reined in, in the half-dusk, sat for a long moment frowning and considering his thoughts. He looked down the dug mule trail by which the other man had vanished, and then again at the shed with its broken, gaping windows and sagging door. Saddle leather creaked as he came down ponderously. A gun slipped into his fingers but then he shoved it back, deciding he would have no need for one.

He entered the building, took a look around in the gloom. He walked over to the stove, glanced into it at evidences of a recent fire. He ran a hand across the table top and looked at his fingers. There was dust but only such as might have accumulated in a few days' time; it was not the grime of years.

He spoke aloud, his voice a rumble in the room as he uttered half-framed thoughts. "If I thought that gunslinger was playing a fast game with me —" But then he shook his grizzled head, puzzlement weighting him. "It don't add!" he grumbled, still aloud. "Still, he's a damned deep one. . . ."

Tyler Gentry returned to his waiting horse. He was a sorely puzzled man.

Chapter Eight

It was late, but lights still burned in the Great Western office. Dan Temple, riding past on his way to the Ramsey place, knew he needed to go no further. Woodenly, he dismounted and tied his lathered sorrel, and stood a moment in the chill darkness preparing himself for what was ahead of him.

Night and town were soundless, under the overcast. Dan's own footsteps scraped loudly as he crossed the cinders and tried the closed, shade-drawn door. He entered; the main room was empty, but beyond the doorway of Abel Ramsey's private office a second lamp burned. Ramsey was there, at his father's old desk, elbows propped upon it and head dropped into his hands.

He raised a haggard face as Dan pushed through the swinging gate and strode back to stand before the desk looking down at him. In the yellow lamplight, Temple's own face was gaunted and drawn from long hours in saddle; its beard-stubbled creases were etched in dust, and dust lay upon his clothing. Broad shoulders dropping tiredly, Dan Temple said, "You know?"

Ramsey nodded. "A rider came through and brought word, three hours ago. We sent up for Stacey's body and what was left of the rig. Nothing more we could do."

A savage anger took Dan Temple suddenly, made him slam his hat against the floor. He turned away a couple of steps, came back smearing a sleeve across the dirt that caked his stubbled cheeks. "Damn it," he cried, "sometimes I wonder how stupid I can be! After the big way I talked last night — and now, for this to happen —"

Ramsey shrugged tiredly. "Forget it! Naturally, nobody's going to hold you to that guarantee. I approved the plan you offered; that makes it my responsibility. Don't blame yourself."

He spoke in a dead and lifeless tone, but something in the words made Dan Temple stop and stare at the man, not quite believing. This wasn't at all what he had expected. Ramsey, he had thought, would have taken the chance to load all the blame onto another's shoulders — would have gone into a weak rage and hurled vituperations at him, for suggesting the plan that had gone foul.

Dan had prepared himself for a disgusting, evil sort of scene; yet nothing of the kind was taking place. And, astonished, he found himself thinking: There must be a backbone in him somewhere, after all. And it's taken a string of disasters to bring it out!

What he said was, "I still blame myself. Such little reputation as I had left was behind the promise I made Evans — and this shoots it full of holes!" He added, "What does Evans say now? Has he heard?"

"He was here, about an hour since. Reed Lawler had been pouring the heat on him, and he broke Evans down. Starting the first of the month, all syndicate business is switching to Lawler's company!"

"The damn fool!" Dan, his temper gone ragged, couldn't hold back the steaming epithet. "Can't he see Lawler is behind all our trouble — that this is the very thing he's been working for?"

Ramsey shot him a close look. "You actually believe that?"

"I damn well know it. I've known it from the first!"

"But it's not a thing you could prove."

Dan Temple thought this over. "I suppose not," he admitted; and, after a moment: "What happens next?"

Ramsey pushed back from the desk, ran a

hand through uncombed hair. "That's not hard to figure. The syndicate has been our largest single account, and losing it will go far toward crippling us. Other business will follow Evans — it's bound to." A twisted, humorless smile quirked the man's tired face. "I'm not kidding myself. Great Western has gone down and down, since the old man died. I've done the best I could but I'm not big enough for this chore — not even with Stella pushing me. And everyone else knows it as well as I do. This is just a quick and merciful way of finishing me off!"

Temple had never thought that he would find himself defending this man, but now he said, "Nonsense! All you need is time to grow into the job. You've had too much thrown at you, all at once. Your father should have known he couldn't live forever, and taken more trouble to train you. Given another year —"

"But I don't get that other year," Abel Ramsey pointed out, quietly. "I'm through — right now! Tonight!"

He really believed this, it was plain, and there was no answer Temple could make. Thoughtfully, Dan leaned for the Stetson he'd thrown down. Holding it, he said slowly, "I guess, then, you don't figure there's anything more I can do for you?"

"No," said Ramsey. He hitched to his feet, chair legs scraping the floor. His next words were not easy ones, but he found the strength to say them. "This looks like the end. . . . There's been trouble between the two of us, Dan, and I'm sorry for my part in it. Thanks for trying to help. I'll have Paul Becker figure your check, first thing in the morning."

" 'Sall right," said Dan, gruffly. "You can send it to the ranch." He turned, about to leave, when an idea jarred him and he hesitated, hauled up by the prodding of it. He said, unexpectedly, "Becker — where does he stay? I got something I want to see him about."

Ramsey showed his surprise, but he answered, "Why, he lives in that rooming house two blocks up the street. Mrs. Handman's place."

Dan knew the house. He nodded and said, "Thanks." He went out briskly, dragging on his battered hat, his boot heels pounding echoes through the empty building.

Mrs. Handman's was dark, but an insistent rapping at the front door brought the woman to open it, a lamp in one hand, the other clutching a wrapper tightly about her. "What do you want?" she demanded. And when he told her: "But everyone's asleep!

158

Can't you wait until tomorrow morning?"

"No," he said. "Which is Becker's room? I'll get him up myself."

"Well, don't rouse the others," she said crossly.

Temple climbed to the second floor and found the room. After a moment the clerk opened the door to him, stared out of eyes blurred with sleep. Dan Temple told him briskly, "Get some clothes on, fellow. You're needed down at the freight yard."

"Me?" The stupid expression of half-waking gave place to a puzzled suspiciousness. "Why would they want me there? And why send you after me, Temple?"

"Time for questions later!" snapped the other. "You better start moving — it's damned important."

One further challenging look and the clerk turned away, leaving the door open so that he could dress by the seepage of light from the hall lamp. Temple leaned against the jamb, waiting for Becker to drag on his clothing. Even so, the man dressed with his usual meticulous neatness, in Eastern-cut suitcoat and trousers and low, lace shoes; his only concession to haste lay in omitting the four-in-hand necktie he usually wore. He came out finally, closing the door, and Temple ushered him down the steps and into the cold, damp darkness of the street.

Here the clerk had more questions that Dan refused to answer, and they went on through the sleeping town — an odd pair, the one slight of build and neatly dressed, the other big and unshaven and dirty enough in trail-stained range clothing. And thus they came to the sprawling bulk of the Ramsey wagon yard, with the big freight wagons lined within and the long, dark barn from which rose the smell and sound of horses. All here was quiet, dark save for a single lantern at the barn entrance.

One glance, and Paul Becker swung about to face his companion. "What joke is this?" he gritted harshly. "Why did you bring me here, anyway?"

"To ask a few questions!" replied Dan Temple, his manner gone hard and dangerous. "And you're going to answer them!"

At something in his voice the other man started to move away; instantly Temple's hand settled on his shoulder, in a grip that Becker could not shake loose. There was the whisper of metal against holster leather as the gun slipped into Temple's other hand. Dan said, "Watch it, fellow! And don't try making a noise. There's nobody around except the Ramsey's watchman, and he's too deaf to hear you."

160

The menace of the gun had quieted Becker. His body stiff under the grip of Temple's fingers, he said icily, "All right. What is it you think you want from me?"

"First, we'll just step back where there's less chance of being interrupted."

Still gripping the bony shoulder, he shoved his man against the rough board fence and along the side of the wagon yard, through high weeds that grew thick in the vacant lot adjoining. Here, some hundred yards from the street, they were in shadow; yet the glow of the lantern, burning over the big double door of the stock barn just across the fence, laid a faint luminescence around them and picked out the features of the men, dimly. Becker's sharp and sullen eyes were dark holes in the pale blob of his face as he stood with his back against the splintery fence boards, head lowered a little, facing Temple and waiting for whatever was going to come.

"All right," said Dan, tightly. "You can start talking, now. I want the truth — all of it — about you and Reed Lawler!"

He heard the other man's sharp drag of breath. "Lawler!" It was a gusty explosion. "Why, you must be out of your head. I don't even know Lawler — never spoken to him."

"Oh, I think so," replied Dan coldly. "It's got to be you. I've gone over the thing a hundred times. There's a leak inside Great Western somewhere — someone who tipped our hand to Lawler about that shipment this afternoon, and got it stolen. You're the key man, Becker. I don't think I have to look any further."

"The charge is ridiculous!" snapped the clerk. "I've got nothing to say to it — or to you either!"

Dan hit him. He didn't put all the weight of his shoulder behind the blow but it was enough to jar the man, to drive his head back with a hard thud against the fence. Temple lifted the fist then and held it level to Becker's eyes. He said, "You had better change your mind about that. You think you're a pretty superior animal, I guess; but all the supercilious pride in the world can't keep me from knocking the spit out of you!"

For a moment the threat, hotly spoken, lay between them. Becker, braced against the fence, stared at the fist cocked and ready to strike again. A thin, black line of blood formed across the man's cheek, and a slow trickle began there and coursed down his face, unhindered and vaguely visible in the poor light.

Dan Temple prodded him. "You ready to talk?"

The man's thin chest lifted on a shuddering, indrawn breath. "You stupid thug!" The words snapped, freighted with icy hatred and contempt. "That's all you know, isn't it — fists and guns? You think if you beat and smash a man enough you can get him to admit anything — any wild notion you've worked up in your own thick skull."

Despite himself, Dan felt something run cold and hollow inside him at these words. From somewhere he seemed to hear an echo of them — what was it? Then he remembered: Vern Jackman's sardonic voice speaking in the silence of the abandoned mine shed. *You'll never be anything but a mugg, Dan. You haven't got the brains for anything but gun-throwing. . . .*

Now, behind the scorn of Paul Becker's lashing words, he recognized the true ring of sincerity. He knew the man was telling the truth; he had tried to reason through the clue in Jackman's scrawled pencil note, but reasoning was not his natural field and somehow, thickheadedly, he had stumbled upon a grievous error.

He looked at the man he had hit, saw the scorn in Paul Becker's eyes. His doubled fist eased open and fell at his side. Dan said, slowly, "You really hate me, don't you? You've hated me from the beginning."

"Yes!" The man's hurled answer was

fierce, bitter. "Because I hate brute power — the unreasoning strength that can smash to pieces in a day what intelligence labors for a year to build. Put a gun in the hands of an ape, and what chance is there for intelligence?"

Becker said this and then winced, visibly, waiting for another retaliating blow in return for his daring. It didn't come. Dan Temple could only stare at the other man, the violence drained out of him, the six-shooter hanging forgotten in his hand. He had not suspected the roiling, leashed emotions that lay beneath the Easterner's cold exterior. He had known that Becker had little use for him, but it had never come clear, before this moment, how deep that loathing went.

He lifted a hand, ran the knuckles slowly across the sharp stubble of his jawbone. He said, gruffly, "I dunno. I been called a number of things in my time but never an ape, that I remember. Maybe, from your point of view, you're right. I never had any schooling to speak of. The folks died early and I went on my own. I learned to use a gun and to slug my way in and out of trouble, and that's about all I did learn. You've probably read more book in a year than I have in my whole lifetime — that's a habit you get young, I suppose, or you never get it at all."

Dan shrugged, while the man against the fence held his silence. "Well, I've made a try or two lately at using my brains and only made a fool of myself — like tonight. And I've learned my lesson." He added, "You can forget about hating me, because I won't be bothering you again. I've succeeded in ruining the Ramseys, and after this I quit. I'm going back to my ranch and this time I'll stay there. It's lucky I've at least got a strong back!"

And with no more than that, he shoved his sixgun into holster and turned away. He saw Paul Becker's hat, that had tumbled to the ground when Dan hit him. He picked this up and handed it to the man. After that, and not waiting for the man to answer, he was gone. He could feel the Easterner's eyes upon his back as he strode away through the weeds of the lot and lost himself in the shadows beside the wagon yard fence. With the burden of this terrible day upon him, Dan Temple was a humbled and weary man.

Nevertheless, he was not through with the Ramseys and he knew this. After all, there was Stella. You couldn't turn your back on a girl like that — much less forget her and the few moments of intimacy that had been between them. Furthermore, there was Wednesday night.

He hadn't seen or heard from her; chained to his homestead, immersed in the healing forgetfulness of physical toil, he saw the passing of the days and wondered, as the time drew nearer, if she remembered the promise she'd extracted from him. Maybe, after what had happened, she no longer cared about the dance or wanted him to take her. Still, it was for her to decide.

A mingled anticipation and uneasiness joined in him as the time approached when he was to see her again. On Wednesday he quit work early, and took special pains in preparing for the ride to town. He had nothing but his work clothes to wear but he put on a clean shirt and jeans and a new, bright neck scarf. He labored over his old Stetson, trying to beat some semblance of shape into its broken brim, replacing the sweated band with a new one he had fashioned out of horsehair. The daylight hours were growing longer. There was still a stain of sunset in the sky as he rode into Dragoon, and found the town unnaturally alive with ranch people already coming in for the dance.

By the time he had seen to his horse and found a place to eat in one of the town's eat

166

shacks, the darkening streets were noisy with the flow of men and women dressed for the occasion. The two saloons and the hotel bar were busy, a constant tide of boisterous men keeping the batwings in motion. This welcome release from the boredom of ranch life had spirits high, friend calling to friend in the settling dusk that shrouded the streets. But Dan Temple was not a part of this, and he drew no more than a curt nod or two as he passed someone he knew, moving along the hard pathways toward the big Ramsey place behind its pickets.

Stella herself opened to him, and as the light from the hall spilled out onto the dark porch he could only stand for a moment, and look at her speechless, his big hat in his hands. She was dressed for the dance, in a gown that was new to Dan Temple. It would have to be green, of course, to do full justice to her eyes, to her rich, piled-up hair, to the flawless texture of her skin. But Dan Temple had never seen a shade of such vibrant warmth, or a gown so cut to accent the perfection of the girl's tall and exquisitely proportioned figure. A collar of green stones lay against her bare throat, and she had heightened artfully the color of her cheeks and of her generous, smiling mouth. She said, "Don't you approve, Dan?"

He told her, "You're very beautiful." And then, as he stepped into the hall and the door with its stag of colored glass swung shut behind him, Stella Ramsey was in his arms and they kissed, slowly and lingeringly, the breath of her parted lips warm upon his own and her body, her long legs pressed hard against him. After that she broke away, with a laugh, and they passed on into the living room. Dan dropped his old Stetson on the table by the archway.

"I hadn't anything to dude up in," he told her. "I'm afraid we'll make a strange pair." He added, after a second's pause while he sought the right words to say it in, "I — wasn't sure you would still want to go."

She faced him directly. "Why not go, Dan? Or had you changed your mind about it?"

"Not me!" he assured her quickly. "I'll be very proud. But — things have changed, since a week ago. I thought maybe the dance wouldn't be — important to you, any more, not after the other things that have happened."

She closed her eyes, shaking her head a little. A shadow of tiredness went across her lovely face. "Dan, if you only knew!"

Then, abruptly, before he could find an answer, she swung away and moved toward a carved monstrosity of a mahogany sideboard. "A drink?" She brought him back a glass, and he watched her movements as she filled it for him from a crystal decanter. He thanked her, and held the drink in his hand, his grave look upon her face.

"Has it been bad, Stella?"

"What would you think? Watching everything crumble, watching it go — even this house I always thought I hated. . . . Our orders canceling, stampeding to Lawler's new outfit. Men saying on the streets and in the bars that Ramsey blood thinned to water in one generation. And Abel —"

"How is he, Stella?"

She set the heavy decanter upon the table beside her. She stood looking at the dark, polished surface of the massive piece of furniture. "You know, Dan, it's very strange. Now that it's too late — now that the worst has happened — he surprises me. He's more levelheaded and stronger than I've ever known him." Her shoulders lifted, and fell again. "Why couldn't he have been like this when there was a need for it? When there was still time to accomplish something — ?"

Dan finished his drink, and put down the empty glass. He had needed the whiskey, to brace him for the next thing he must say.

"I'll always blame myself, of course, for the mistake that lost you the Evans account."

"What good is blaming?" she said, shaking her head. "It would have happened. They were determined to break us. What good — ?" Suddenly she lifted the decanter, ran whiskey into Dan's empty glass and, snatching the drink, downed it quickly. She made a bitter face over it and then looked at Dan — half-ashamed, half-challenging.

"You don't like to see a woman drink, do you?" she demanded. "But I had to, tonight. Because, I'm going to that dance — no matter what it does to me. I'm going to look them in the face, and defy them all. Let them talk about me, let them think what they like. I won't be crushed! Not by these trivial people. At least, I have that much of my father's strength!"

"Please!" he exclaimed, helpless and unhappy in the face of her mood.

She smiled again, quickly, but the smile did not touch her eyes. She put a hand on his. "I'm sorry. Don't mind how I act. Just help me, if you can — help me to get through this evening, one way or another." Her shoulders straightened, her head lifted.

"We might as well be starting," she said, firmly. "I'll fetch my wrap. . . ."

The Oddfellows' Hall was already alive

with activity, with rigs and saddle horses lining the hitch rails solidly in front of it, and a flow of new arrivals passing inside and up narrow stairs to the second floor where colored lights and the uncertain sounds of fiddles tuning issued through the opened windows. The usual crowd of unattached men and half-grown boys loitered about the entrance, to hooraw their friends going in with girls on their arms. A half-empty bottle passed the rounds. A dog, touched with the unaccustomed excitement, snapped at the patient horses at the rail, darted silently in to sniff polished boots and to bark idiotically at every raucous outburst of male laughter.

As Dan Temple came toward this scene with Stella beside him, he braced himself for trouble. By her defiant attitude toward the town and its judgment, by her wearing of this gown, she was inviting it; but he said nothing, though for just an instant he knew a flash of resentment.

If trouble came, he would have to settle it. Surely she realized this. But when he glanced at her, moving beside him with head erect and hand tight within the crook of his elbow, such vague emotions fled him and he could think only: It's hard enough for her! She is doing the only thing she feels can be done, and it's up to me to see it through. . . .

Then they had reached the lighted building and the beginnings of ribald comment were instantly silenced as Dan Temple lifted his head and his hard, challenging look showed beneath shadowing Stetson brim. The knot of loungers froze in sudden silence.

Through it the two of them passed, Stella with a dainty hand drawing her skirt aside to prevent its brushing the muddy boots of a gaping cowpuncher.

A man stood in the doorway, unintentionally blocking it, half-rolled cigarette forgotten in his hands. Dan Temple stopped in front of this man and said, "Do you mind — ?"

Hastily, the puncher mumbled something and pulled aside, spilling his tobacco; he stood pressed against the wall as Dan handed Stella up the two brief steps and then followed her through the opening and climbed the steep and narrow flight of stairs beyond.

Once in a while, it seemed, a reputation like his could serve some purpose after all!

After that they were on the second floor, and from beyond the door of a small check room came the soft glow of colored lanterns, the sound of gay talk and busy movement, and — precisely now — the striking up of the first set. Dan checked his hat and Stella's shawl with the pimpled lad at the checking table, got a ticket for them. Gunbelts hung from nails fastened in the wall behind the desk, but Dan had left his weapon at the ranch.

The first couples were straggling out onto the high-waxed floor as he escorted Stella through the wide doorway. Dim lantern light fell on bright, colored streamers, on range folk uncommonly well-dressed for the occasion, on the two fiddlers and the guitarist and the accordion-player who were still feeling each other out through the uncertain measures of the opener. Dan, determined not to make an entrance of this, had an arm around Stella's waist almost before she was prepared, and had swept her off among the other gliding couples. Even so, as the big room gyrated about them, he was keenly conscious of the quick attention that centered upon them although individual faces were lost to him in the uncertain lighting.

You could not long keep men's eyes from Stella — not this evening, not in that bright gown, that accented the striking beauty of her and the perfection of her throat and the arm that lay against Dan's shoulder.

Yet, while the music continued, he could forget the others in the pleasure of her nearness, the warm curve of her waist beneath his hand, the scent of her. Her eyes and red lips smiled up at him from a face flushed by the dancing, yet there was a kind of desperation in the smile. And when at last the music stopped, and reluctantly Dan released her and they stepped apart, the rest of the room took on reality.

Not an eye there, he thought, but was watching them with hostility or mockery or simply plain cold interest. He swung around, singling out faces he knew, showing them that their stares meant nothing to him. Among the rest he met the cold, unyielding regard of old Mark Chess; beside his boss stood Tom McNeil, uncomfortable in a suitcoat that appeared not to belong to him, and a frozen hostility seemed to crackle as both men's eyes locked briefly with Temple's. He hunted for Ruth then, found her talking earnestly with a sunburned cowpuncher from her father's ranch. She didn't meet his look, but he had the feeling that she had only turned away a second before it touched her.

Stella Ramsey said, in a small voice, "Just look, Dan! This is Dragoon — these are the petty, evil-minded sort of people we live with!"

"Do you want to go?" he asked.

"I do not! Why give in to them? Oh — there's the music, starting."

That stiff defiance hardening the edge of her smile and her too-bright eyes, she tossed her magnificent copper curls and came again into his arms. But this time there was, for him, no ignoring the rest of the room; there was no pleasure in the music or the lightness of her body in his arms.

They ended near the refreshment table and he took Stella over there for a glass of punch. A ranchwoman drew back, all too quickly, and though the table was busy they found no trouble locating a place. Expressionless, Dan scooped up the drinks for them both. All about them friends were chatting in a pleasant hubbub of voices, but these two had nobody to talk with but each other; and Dan was past words now, his jaw clamped hard, a dangerous light beginning to flicker in back of his narrowing gray eyes.

A voice said, "Gimme the honor of the next one, lady?"

He was a red-faced, grinning cowhand, sweaty of face and a little abashed at his own audacity. Beyond him Dan caught sight of a group of men that had their heads

175

together, watching. They'd put their friend up to this, no doubt, and the glassiness of his blue eyes hinted that it had taken a little bravemaker out of a bottle to bring him to the point of trying.

Dan said, "Beat it, fellow!"

"Let him alone, Dan!" Stella told him, quickly, and she turned an artificial smile upon the man. "Certainly you may have the dance. Thank you for asking me."

And a moment later she was gone, in the dazed puncher's awkward embrace. Dan stood where he was, not quite believing, but reading correctly the false smile frozen upon her lips. This, too, was a part of her defiance, but he knew what would follow.

Those other cowhands yonder, showing now a stupified amazement at their friend's success, would soon be emboldened themselves to the point of cutting in. The thing would become a rowdy joke. She'd have her partners, all right, but not the kind she wanted. No respectable townsman — no one with a name to protect or the dread of a wife's anger to hamper him — would dance with Stella Ramsey tonight, despite the inviting and dangerous charms of the brilliant gown.

Dan felt an access of pity for her. And as he turned away, his resentment toward these smug people was near passing the bounds of endurance.

CHAPTER NINE

He caught sight of Ruth Chess, alone for the moment, and on an obscure impulse he turned and strode over toward where she stood. She must have sensed his coming but did not look at him until he was beside her and spoke; he saw the grip she took upon herself then before she tilted her head, slowly, and lifted a face toward him that was carefully expressionless.

"Yes?" she said, in a voice that sounded not too sure of itself.

In that moment, he found himself noting the sharp contrast between Stella Ramsey and this girl. They were really nothing alike, and the differences ran deep. Since that unfortunate removal from the St. Louis of her childhood, Stella had never known the inner assurance of belonging anywhere. Ruth Chess, for her part, had grown up on a ranch; she had known no other life nor wanted any. She had contentment; and Dan realized, in his quick flash of intuition, that this was the reason for her own calm and quiet adjustment to life, which the Ramsey girl had never achieved.

Tonight she was dressed simply but becomingly in a plain blouse and skirt he had seen on her any number of times before. Her sundarkened skin wore a look of utter cleanness and health. Her dark hair had been neatly brushed, caught up with a white satin ribbon; this one small touch was all the trimming she needed, and it seemed utterly fitting to her nature. She wore, of course, no coloring; and as a result the sudden pallor of her sunbrowned cheeks was all the more evident as she faced Dan Temple.

He thought she knew what he was going to ask, and was pleading silently for him not to say it. But he wouldn't let her off. "Dance with me, Ruth?"

She hesitated. Past her, he caught sight of Mark Chess, face thunderous as he started forward plainly intent on taking his daughter away from Dan. But then the girl nodded and, without speaking, lifted her arms to him. Dan took her and they moved out upon the floor.

Stella's gown flashed yonder among the drab ranch dresses and homespun jeans; she was in the arms of a second cowpuncher, by this time, and Dan glimpsed her set and desperate look as they swirled past. Immediately she was swept away and lost to him, and Dan was alone again with his own partner.

He had never held Ruth Chess before and had not realized just how small she was. She came hardly to his shoulder; yet she had the feel of solidness and strength. He blurted suddenly, "I've been wanting to talk to you about — about a lot of things. But the last time we met you walked away from me. . . ."

He couldn't tell that she had even heard him. She said nothing; he could see no more than the top of her brown head, bent so that it all but touched the rough material of his jacket. Doggedly, Dan persisted: "I dunno what you likely think of me, by now. If you figure I'm a damned fool, I'll admit you're probably more or less right after the way I bungled things for the Ramseys. But this other business — I thought you were enough a friend of mine, Ruth, that you wouldn't believe an irresponsible rumor. . . ."

Suddenly, when she still refused to answer, he broke step and, there in a backwash of dancers at the edge of the floor, seized the girl by her shoulders. "Ruth!" he insisted, as the rest of the couples moved past. "Look at me!"

She tried to pull away from him, her face still averted. Dan put a hand beneath her chin and lifted her face until he could see the tears shining on her cheeks.

"Please!" she moaned, chokingly. "Isn't it enough to use me for a — a —" Her voice broke apart completely then and she stood before him, weeping openly. And only then did Dan Temple recognize the callousness of the thing he had done to her.

He dropped his hands. "I'm sorry," he muttered; but apology couldn't help.

It couldn't compensate for his forcing himself on her, knowing she wouldn't refuse him — deliberately counting on her good reputation to help remove some of the stigma he bore in the eyes of these other people. He saw, now, it had been a cruel and unfeeling exploitation of her friendship.

"You're right," he muttered bleakly. "I'm no rotten good — and you've no reason to put up with me. I won't bother you any more!"

He heeled away quickly, so she would not have to answer, and strode directly across the waxed floor, working through the dancers until he found Stella Ramsey. It was not hard to locate her. She made the center, just then, of an argument between a couple of admirers — two half-drunken cowhands, each holding her by an arm and trying to get rid of the other so as to have her for himself. Various shades of amusement or disgust showed in the bystanders who happened to be watching the thing. Then Dan Temple walked in, thrusting his wide-shouldered shape between the two quarreling men, and he said sharply, "All right, boys! Blow!"

He only united them against himself; they turned on him and their shouting voices were enough to drown the whining of the fiddles, and draw now the attention of the entire room. But the cowpunchers were not too drunk to recognize Dan Temple; as they saw who it was they all at once subsided, making a quick stumbling retreat. Dan turned to Stella Ramsey.

"I'm taking you home!" he told her flatly.

She flared at him: "You are not!" Dan, past arguing now, reached to take her wrist but she jerked away, face flushed with the beginning of anger. "Let me alone!"

"No!" This time he managed to catch hold of her and his hand tightened, inexorably.

"We've made enough of a spectacle here," he said. His own temper was slipping fast. She continued to resist him, trying to tear loose from his firm grip on her arm. Seeing every eye in the place centered on them, Dan knew only a desperate desire to drag her away from there, to cut this nightmare scene short before it could go any longer.

His voice louder than he intended, he gritted, "By God, I say you're coming with me!"

Someone behind them remarked, in a tone of heavy amusement, "Better go on. You ought to know you can't stir a man up and expect him to wait indefinitely —"

Stella's wrist slipped unhindered from Dan's fingers. Slowly, a strange trembling in every limb, he came about and saw, through a white blaze of fury, the sardonic face of Reed Lawler. For a moment Dan stood still — poised, tensed, all attention narrowing to a point of hating fury on that too-handsome, too-virile face. In his ears a buzzing drowned all other noises; the squawk of the fiddles, the hum of excited voices, came dimly, blanketed by this.

As from a great distance away, he heard someone cry out suddenly, hysterically, "Fight! *Fight!*"

Then his legs were propelling him forward, and his fist was swinging for Lawler's jaw. He felt it strike, felt the stabbing jolt of it run up his stiffened arm. But he had telegraphed the attack and before he could recover from his forward lunge a retaliating blow struck him behind the ear, rocking him. It filled his head with explosive pain, but at the same time cleared it of mere blind emotion; it turned him into a clear-thinking, clean-functioning machine. And when Lawler tried to follow with a second short, chopping drive Dan blocked it, countering with a hard right of his own.

Lawler went down, hard. He had forgotten the icy slickness of the waxed floor and he lost his footing and landed in a sprawl, spinning half around while men and women yelled and scrambled clear and with a smash the table that held the punch bowl toppled. Lawler's coat had fallen open. Dan saw that the man had left off his underarm holster and, satisfied to know this, waited for him to fight back to his feet.

Then Lawler was up and they charged at each other again, fists working, slugging it out.

Reed Lawler didn't look particularly hard, but he was. He had size and solid weight and he was a disciplined, tough fighter. He yielded nothing. He seemed as eager for this as Dan Temple; oddly enough, his eyes behind the blond hair that strung into his sweaty face appeared to hold real hatred.

The combatants fought their way through the uproar of the milling, screaming crowd, surging back and forth with onlookers scattering out of the way. It was damnably hard to maneuver on that wax-slick dance floor. Dan lost his balance once and, doubled over like that, took a sledging wallop on the back of the neck that puts stars rocketing across his vision. But he recovered and a moment later sent Lawler backward into a ceiling upright. Lawler pivoted around it, pawing for support. He caught a handful of bunting as he went sprawling and tore it down, setting a colored lantern to swaying grotesquely overhead. Its shadowy light rocked back and forth across the scattering crowd below.

Dan, panting with exertion, heard someone yell: "Can't anybody put an end to this? Why don't they fetch the sheriff — ?"

He waded in again, then, as Reed Lawler rose and squared around to meet him. Both men had blood on them, their clothing torn and sweated through. Evenly matched, neither showed signs of yielding though the battle was wearing them both down, pouring out their stamina in a mutual hatred that was at last finding outlet.

They reached the raised musician's stand and Dan found himself trapped there. A blow spilled him across it; the orchestra scattered wildly to the accompaniment of a long-drawn squawk from the accordion-player's dangling instrument. Before Dan could right himself Lawler was upon him, and big hands were tearing at his throat. Lawler's panting breath came hot upon his bloody, sweat-streaming face.

For a moment Dan Temple thought he was not going to break free. The fingers at his throat seemed tightened into iron-hard bands and he tore at them futilely, with strength that drained out of him as his trapped lungs fought for air. But then he got a knee lifted and he straightened it with a pistoning lift that flung his enemy from him, and before Lawler could recover Dan had gained his feet again. He was really tiring now. His legs had turned shaky under him and it was like wading through water to reach the other man and start the pounding again.

His arm was back, cocked, when a hand grabbed it and a voice bawled hysterically: "Stop this, d'you hear? Stop it! You're wrecking the place!" Dan turned to snarl at the man, dragging his arm free. And at that moment Lawler hit him on the side of the head, crushingly. Dan went under.

He lay in a forest of legs, dazed by the blow. Shaking his head to get the dizziness out of it, he looked for Lawler. Yonder there was a glimpse of the man's shoulders. Reed Lawler had suddenly made up his mind to end this by getting out of it; while his enemy lay dazed for the moment he was heading for the far doorway, fast.

Grunting something unintelligible, Dan shoved to his feet and went after him, clawing a way through the crowd. He caught up with Lawler on the stairs that led down from the little check room outside and, hardly thinking, took off from the head of the flight. He struck Lawler in mid-air, in a low tackle; they went down that way, a lashing tangle of bodies.

Dan was the first on his feet. He waited and when Lawler came pulling himself up the edge of the door at the foot of the dark stairs, grabbed the man and helped him erect, then slammed a fist into the center of his face and sent him reeling drunkenly out into the street. And Dan went after him.

Here there was still another crowd that split noisily away from the door as the men hurtled through. Their shouting started the horses at the tie-up to circling in fright. Dan got to Lawler, found him glassy-eyed and wobbly. He was badly enough beaten, himself, but the full measure of his hatred hadn't worked itself out yet and he went ahead, swinging, right and left — slow, sledging blows that met no opposition now from his enemy. For Lawler was done. His bloody head rocked to one side and then the other, as Temple punished him along the front of the building, and the blows were

186

payment for what this man had done to Dan, and to the Ramseys; also, they were a release for the emotions that had been pent up within him during all these troubled days since Lawler's coming.

Then Reed Lawler dropped at his feet and lay moaning feebly; and at last Dan was ready to quit. He leaned a shoulder against the wall, panting hoarsely. He spat into the earth, wiped a palm across his cheek and looked at the blood, and spat again. The taste in his mouth was brassy. Within him there was a half-formed question, that took shape only slowly: Why the hell did Lawler fight like that? What kept him going? He'd already ruined me; what reason was there for him to hate me so strong?

He gave it up and lifted his head shakily to stare about him in returning awareness of his surroundings.

The crowd that had been making a racket moments before was strangely still now, and they were keeping their distance. Dan Temple remembered, dully that the sheriff had been sent for. He didn't want a brush with Tyler Gentry just now, over something that was none of the law's business. He pushed away from the front wall of the building, and moved uncertainly toward the entrance. And the mob drew back.

It looked a long way to the top of the dark stairs, and besides they were jammed solid with men who'd stampeded down from the dance hall overhead. As Dan halted, a hand placed against the jamb to brace him, someone in the mob said gruffly, "If you're looking for your lady friend, she run out on you, mister. She beat it right after the fight started."

Dan Temple looked around for the speaker but couldn't locate him. His vision and his very thought processes were groggy with tiredness and the aftermath of the punishment he'd taken. But he decided after a long, slow minute's consideration that what he'd been told was apparently the truth; so he turned away, and the crowd on the pathway separated for him.

He left that place, made off alone into the night with an uncertain step; the crisp coolness, touching his bruised and sweaty body, helped quickly to wipe some of the tired fogginess out of his brain. By the time he climbed the hill to the big Ramsey house, he had pretty well recovered although there was still a bone-deep weariness in him.

The big house with its scrollwork trimming was dark behind its pickets, save for a dim light in the hall. Dan Temple went up on the porch and pulled the bell cord, and waited. He got no answer. He tried to peer in through the colored glass of the stag window but could see no movement. After a moment he turned away, feeling a kind of relief even though he knew Stella must be inside there, refusing to open to him. He didn't feel up to confronting Stella, after what had happened; she had been the cause of the trouble and he was nearly as angry with her as with himself. If they met now there might be harsh things said, weary accusations that would later be regretted, but past retracting then.

Only, something told him that there wouldn't be any later. This tonight was the finish of everything. He had tried fitting himself into an alien way of life but after the spectacle he'd just made of himself in front of the town there would be no convincing anyone he could ever belong here — that he could ever be anything but the mugg Vern Jackman had once called him.

He thought, wearily: The hell with it! The hell even with the ranch, with this whole abortive effort toward respectability and a better way of life. He should have taken the easier way, gone on along that other path his feet were already well accustomed to, and spared himself all this wasted time and useless effort.

Well, at least, you could always change back! Heading for the stable and his bay gelding, Dan Temple told himself the experiment was ended, and none too soon. He had finally learned his lesson. He would shake off respectability like an ill-fitting garment; and tomorrow the old trails would claim him. . . .

Reed Lawler was never entirely sure how he got back to his room, in a converted cubbyhole at the rear of the new stage line headquarters. He remembered waving aside the proffered help of those who had put him on his feet after that crushing battle with Temple; he was contemptuous of aid, sure of his ability to navigate despite the beating he'd taken. But apparently he demanded more than his battered body could give, because the next he knew he was lying on the rumpled cot, in darkness, and without any memory of how he got there.

For a long time he lay, too hurt to move, while a welter of humiliating and painful images slid through his dazed mind. Who would have thought Temple would be so hard to lick! More than that, who would have imagined himself losing his head and getting mixed up in such a shameful brawl? It had been the whiskey he'd drunk that did the talking, he supposed — that, and some obscure, not-understood rage, goading him on to put pressure on Temple and force him to fight. Lawler groaned and twisted on the tumbled bedclothes. To be beaten! Nor was that the worst of it. There would be repercussions, plenty of them. He would hear about this later, from the man whose money paid for the job he was doing here in Dragoon. There would be scenes he didn't now like to contemplate.

These bleak thoughts dragged him up off the couch, finally, and sent him stumbling to find the lamp and get it burning. These quarters of his were nothing much, but they were only temporary. They smelled of raw lumber and sawdust and paint, from the recently completed remodeling of the old building which was now headquarters of the new freighting company he had been hired to manage. Lawler squinted at himself in the mirror above the washstand, and cursed painfully.

Temple's fists had done dreadful damage to his rugged good looks; one eye was closed, the face lumpy with bruised swellings and cuts. All the teeth on one side of his jaw ached and he wondered with a cold dread if they had been loosened by the sledging. The worst of the whole thing was that, not remembering anything clearly about the fight, he couldn't even have the satisfaction of knowing what damage he had done to his opponent, except for what could be guessed from the state of his cut and bleeding hands.

His clothing was ruined. Every muscle protesting, he got out of the bloody suitcoat and threw it on the bed, ripped off the shirt, and then poured cold water into the hand-basin and set to work cleaning up. The sting of his cuts made him swear a little. The water in the basin was a pale red when he finished and had used a towel, carefully.

After that, he went across the room to a battered bureau, rummaged and found a clean white shirt. Turning with it in his hands, he halted in astonishment. He had a visitor.

Stella Ramsey had managed somehow to enter the little room without noise, and she stood with her back to the closed door, her shoulders pressed against it. For a moment she said nothing and the silence ran out as Lawler stared, uncomprehending.

She still wore the green dress, but it was crumpled and there was a tear at one knee where she might have caught it on some-thing and jerked it free, unmindful of dam-age. She looked in every way distracted,

192

hardly knowing what she did. Her coppery hair was disarranged; her breast lifted in labored breathing under the scanty bodice of the gown. Her face was white, drawn with some emotion. Only the eyes, seemingly a shade darker than normal, were fiercely alive and glowing as she stood there facing the man who was her enemy.

Lawler was first to find his tongue. "Well!" He tossed aside the shirt, his battered mouth twisted into a sardonic, contemptuous grin. "This is really unexpected! Come to see what your fine friend, Temple, did to me? Or is there a more flattering reason?" He added, viciously: "You can't seem to stay away from men's bedrooms, can you?"

"Go ahead!" she lashed at him; her mouth was a tight red slash against her pallid face, her voice little more than a strangled whisper. "Make your filthy talk! It's the last time you ever will, Lawler. It's the last foul, low thing you'll ever say about me or any woman!"

She showed him the gun, then. She had been holding it at her side, among the full folds of the skirt; now she lifted it, in a white-knuckled, trembling hand. It was a small-caliber, short-snouted revolver; the nickeled barrel gleamed waveringly in the yellow lampglow as she leveled the bore against his naked, yellow-matted chest.

Lawler looked at it, his bruised face gone suddenly expressionless except that a tiny muscle tensed and flickered at the base of his jaw. He said coldly, "You haven't got the nerve!"

"Oh, haven't I!" she cried. "After what you've done? Wrecked my family's fortunes, and then done your best to smear me with the slime of the streets? Small, cheap rumors — yes, I could expect them, in a town like this one, and I would have waited and let them die. Only, you've kept them alive, deliberately — I know that now. I've heard them on your own filthy mouth. And for that, and every other reason — I'm going to kill you, Reed Lawler!"

Still emotionless, he looked at the gun and saw the hammer lift under the pressure of her tightening finger. The muzzle wavered violently; yet at that range, in that tiny room, there was little chance of a bullet failing of its mission. The lamp on the wall bracket flickered a little. Through the half-open window beside them, the distant sounds of the town came on a crisp swirl of night coolness, and faded again.

"All right!" said Lawler. The words were a snarl. His face had altered suddenly, his eyes slitted, his mouth twisted out of shape. "Do it, if you think you can! Just pull the trigger!"

He came toward her, two paces, and the barrel of the gun was a few bare inches from his body. He might have made a sudden move to wrest it from her, but he didn't; he stood with his arms hanging at his sides, his head pulled back, his eyes mere pinpoints stabbing down at her own. A vein throbbed in his sweatbeaded forehead, and the words he shouted at her were hardly more than babblings, making scarcely any sense at all:

"Pull the trigger, damn you! But you won't! You see, it's not your way. You couldn't murder a man. It'd be too clean — too merciful! You'd rather taunt and torment him with someone else, and send him to hell that way. You cheap, nogood —"

"Oh, stop it! *Stop it!*" The outcry was a choked sob of anguish. Suddenly without warning, the gun slipped from her fingers, unfired. For a moment the two of them stood so, without word or movement. Stella's ashen face contorted by a look that should have been loathing hatred but was, oddly, something else.

Suddenly she was in his arms, her own straining tight about him, their mouths hotly and hungrily together. Timeless seconds they clung to each other like that, and then they broke apart and she stumbled back from him. Their eyes met in a distracted, uncomprehending bewilderment.

"Damn you!" Reed Lawler exclaimed, hoarsely. "I'd rather you'd shoot me than this! Why can't you leave me alone?"

A fit of trembling seized her, and she leaned against the door to steady herself. The hand she lifted to push back her tumbled coppery hair was unsure and shaking. "I — I don't —" She tried to summon and organize the confusion of emotions within her. "You've done everything to make me hate you! You've ruined us, you've —"

Lawler put his hands upon her arms, and they were cold to the touch. "I've done only what you made me do! At first it was no more than a matter of business, a job I was hired for. Only I — fell in love with you! I would have called a halt, after that — I would have made them find another man to do their dirty work. But then I learned of you, and Temple — in his room. And I was hurt — crazy mad with jealousy. I determined I'd break you both. . . ."

She shook her head, wearily. "But it wasn't true. Not a word of it true. There's nothing between me and Dan Temple. I think he's in love with me but I've only given him what encouragement I needed to keep him on our side. It was a matter of policy — and I hated it. Don't you believe me?"

There was a long silence. Reed Lawler had calmed a little. His bruised mouth twisted a little, now, into a sardonic and bitter smile. "So it's been a colossal joke, after all — a joke on the two of us! Putting us on opposite sides when all along we were meant to be in love. Because, you do love me. You can't deny it, now!"

"Please!" she moaned. "Let me alone — let me think —"

Instead, he pulled her to him and again they kissed, and her arms were tight about him. As they broke apart she lifted a hand and touched his hurt and swollen cheek. She said: "The brute! Look how he's hurt you —"

"Temple!" Lawler shrugged. "He's nothing but a stupid fool, with hard fists and a talent for gunwork; but how you've made me hate him! Well, we'll forget him now!" He went on quickly, his voice louder with rising emotion. "We'll forget everything that's happened — all the harm I've done. We'll undo all of that! We'll save Great Western!"

"But — how?" she exclaimed. "It's too late — the worst has already happened. There's nothing left to save!"

"You think so?" He laughed, and his eyes gleamed with a secret amusement. "Just give me a chance to show you! Why, with one word I can break wide open the whole scheme to wreck your company — and if you're on the level with me I'll do it. But I've got to be sure of you. If I name the man who hired me for this job, it may mean prison for me before the mess is cleared up — you understand that, don't you? I tell you, if I thought for one moment you weren't playing square with me — that this was just another 'matter of policy' —"

His voice had gone hard, and his look burned into her face. But she was sure of him, now, and sure also of the strange emotion she had found within herself — the perverse fascination in each other that had disguised itself as hatred. She laid her head against his shoulder, a smile on her own red mouth. "You don't need to worry," she murmured. "I'll do anything. Marry you, if you want me. And whatever comes, I'll stand with you. You won't go to prison; Abel and I can see to that."

Convinced, then, of her sincerity, Reed Lawler's arms tightened about her. "All right," he said boldly. "Then I'll talk! It's going to be fun, just watching his face when I blow him out of the water. He thought he was safe — he thought I'd never dare to expose him. But when you know his name —"

There was the sudden, startling smash of a gun, in the darkness just beyond the open window. Stella felt Lawler jerk convulsively. She heard the grunt of exploding breath from him; and then his weight became a drag upon her and in horror she watched him slip out of her arms.

He went to his knees, his head sliding loosely down her long body. His hands groped blindly at her waist, her thighs. Then he was a huddled heap upon the floor and as she stepped away from him, he rolled over face down on the uncarpeted boards. She saw the bullet hole, then, in his naked back beneath the left shoulder blade. She saw the blood; and that was when she screamed. . . .

CHAPTER TEN

The shot and the scream, together, shook that town and stirred it to the core. Within a matter of seconds men were running excitedly among the houses, calling questions, trying to seek out the source of the sounds. Stella Ramsey, unmoving beside Lawler's bleeding body, heard the confused noises but they seemed to come from a great distance; and after the first, throat-tearing shriek of horror she could not have made answer or called for help, even if her numbed brain had prompted her to.

The cries came nearer; running feet crunched on cinders in the alley outside the freight office. A face appeared at the window, briefly — a face with horror scribbled upon it. It stared, wide-eyed, mouth open. Then it jerked away and a frenzied shout went up: "Over here, Sheriff! Hurry!"

More running feet, converging now on that place. And suddenly the door was thrown open under the heavy fist of Tyler Gentry. The sheriff stood with the crowd pressing at his back, and ran his quick, intent scrutiny over the room, his keen glance missing nothing. Over his shoulder he hurled an order at the men outside: "Don't come in here!" And in spite of their eager curiosity there was no one who ventured to disobey him. They fought for vantage points at the door and window but the sheriff entered the room alone, his thin-lipped mouth and hard jaw clamped in unyielding firmness.

And even now Stella Ramsey did not move or tear her eyes from the shape of horror at her feet. The sheriff looked at her, at

Lawler's body. There could be no question that the man was dead. Not touching him, Gentry leaned instead and picked up the fallen gun. He sniffed at the muzzle, a fleeting expression of puzzlement coming into his eyes. He broke the weapon, looked at the loads, and stood a moment weighing the gun in one blocky fist, absorbing the fact that his first quick surmise was wrong and that this weapon had not been fired — was not the one which had done the killing.

He turned to Stella Ramsey, then, and although his face still wore the grim mask of the manhunter his voice was surprisingly gentle, almost kindly. "All right, Stella."

There was a chair handy and he helped her into it; she moved stiffly, without volition. "The bullet came through the window, didn't it?" he suggested. "How much did you see? Do you know who fired it?"

Her eyes still staring, as though sightless, she tried to answer. "I — It wasn't —" She was shaking now, her whole body trembling, and there was no coherence in her fragmentary effort at speech. Tyler Gentry, seeing the futility of prodding, had already turned back to the men in the doorway.

"Somebody had better fetch a doctor — not for Lawler, but the girl. The rest of you, if you can't do any good, you might at least stay the hell away from that window! This is a murder, but if there's any clues left you've probably trampled them all in the mud by now!"

The crowd pulled back hastily at his sharp words, and a couple of the men started off hurriedly on the quest for a doctor. Tyler Gentry turned back into the room, scratching his grizzled head. He looked at Stella and grunted, "I wish you'd try and snap out of this enough to tell me what happened here. What you might have seen through the window —"

"It was awful!" Stella had partially recovered control. She sat huddled in the chair with tight-knuckled hands clutching the sides of the seat; she was disarrayed and wild-eyed and her voice sounded as though her throat were scraped raw by the scream that had been torn from her. But at least she had found coherent speech.

"We were — talking, and the shot —" she shuddered violently as her glance wandered back to the huddled and bloody shape of Lawler, on the uncarpeted floor. "He just — fell, and died. Right in front of my eyes —"

The sheriff said, heavily, "You say you were talking. What about?"

She looked at him. "It had nothing to do

with his being killed."

"I'd rather be the judge of that." Gentry stood shaking his head, his eyes on her white face. He said, with gruff gentleness, "Don't try to hide anything, Stella. It's no good, at a time like this. The law is going to want to know everything. It's gonna want to know what you were doing here, in Lawler's room — and there's no use thinking you can get out of telling the truth!"

Her lips — a harsh red gash against the pallor of her face, now — trembled; but her eyes were bright with anger. "You're going to persecute me? You, Tyler Gentry?"

"It's not me!" he answered, with a gesture of exasperation. "It's my job — a job I have to do. You know I've always stood up for the Ramseys, and I'll do it now — the best I can. But I can't help if you won't do your part by being honest with me! Now, will you answer my question?"

Her glance wavered and broke before his own, but she would not speak. He shrugged and turned away from her. And it was at this moment that excited scuffling sounded in the alleyway; men out there were yelling, cursing, and someone called the sheriff's name. "Come here! We got something for you!"

The light was poor, except for what came

through the door and window. So Sheriff Gentry, striding quickly into the alley, saw at first only a struggling knot of men approaching the office; then he saw that they had a prisoner, and that he was fighting savagely and giving trouble in his efforts to break loose from their hands. The sheriff demanded sharply, "What is this?" and moved forward.

A man said, "We found him hiding in a shed, down the alley. He made a noise and we looked in and found him, and he started fighting like a wildcat!"

"Lemme have a look at him!"

All at once the prisoner, overcome by numbers, subsided. With their hands on him he stood panting, his clothing torn, lank hair tumbled into his bony face. There was blood on him. Someone jerked his head up, limply, and the lamplight from the window struck across him. The man was Abel Ramsey.

The sight of his friend wrung a grunt of astonishment from the lawman. He heard somebody remark: "No gun on him. He must have thrown it away after he killed Lawler."

"I didn't kill him!" cried Ramsey.

"Then what are you doing here? Why should you hide, and put up a fight when we ran across you?"

A kind of sickness crawled through Tyler Gentry as he heard the questions and saw the cold logic behind them. He looked hopelessly at the frightened young man and he said, "You'd better start talking, Abel. It looks awful damn bad, after your trouble with Lawler. I hope you can give a reasonable explanation."

Ramsey answered, leadenly, "I'll talk to you, Sheriff. But not here — not in front of all these others. I can't!"

"Oh." Frowning, Gentry considered this briefly. "All right," he told the men. "Let him go — I'll take the responsibility for him. Lantry," he ordered, singling out one of the crowd, "I'm leaving you in charge here until I get back. Don't let anything be disturbed until the coroner's had his look at the body. I won't be gone more than a few minutes."

"All right, Sheriff."

The doctor who had been sent for came hurrying along the alley then, and Gentry nailed him. "Take a look at the Ramsey girl, see if there's anything you can do for her nerves. She's had a bad shock. Maybe a sedative or something; and then I guess you better take her home." Gentry turned to his prisoner. "You come along, Abel."

"I'd like to see my sister, first."

Gentry hesitated, then shook his head.

"Sorry. Can't take the time now. It'll be best to wait until she gets over the thing a little." Actually, Tyler Gentry wanted to hear Abel Ramsey's story, alone, before Ramsey had a chance to alter it as a result of what the girl might say.

The sheriff didn't like any part of this. He had known these two for a long time, had watched them grow up and mature. He had watched them anxiously during the trying period since their father's death, and especially since the evil days that had fallen upon their freighting business. But now, with this sordid thing tonight, friendship had to be forgotten. He had to remember, now, that he was first of all an officer of the law, and that a serious crime had been committed.

Ramsey went with him without protest, the few blocks to the courthouse. The building was dark except for a lamp in the sheriff's office, where the night jailer was reading a tattered magazine. Gentry sent him out of the room and, bracing his solid frame against the edge of the spur-scarred desk top, told the prisoner, "I want your story now, Abel!"

A tic had formed in the muscles of the other's cheek. It twitched spasmodically as he stood there facing the man who had been his friend. He reached a bony hand to shove the hair out of his wide and staring eyes, and the man trembled. He said, "There — there isn't anything to tell. Except I didn't kill him!"

"What were you doing in the alley?"

His glance flickered, as he quailed before the necessity of answering. Then he drew strength from some reserve and his body straightened; his face, that was bruised and bloody from the fist of one of his captors, settled into firmness.

"I followed my sister there. I was at home, trying to sleep, when she came back to the house by herself and left a moment later. I — I don't know, something alarmed me. I dressed in a hurry and tried to follow her —"

"Just a minute," Gentry cut in on him. "Let's tell the whole story, Abel. What alarmed you was hearing her take your revolver that you kept in that old bureau in the hall — wasn't that it? You got up and looked, and saw the gun was gone. That's the reason you followed!"

Ramsey's eyes flashed briefly, and then the fatigued look came into them again. "All right!" he snapped. "You know too much about our family, Tyler — and now you're turning it against us! All right — she had the gun. But she didn't kill him! I was there, at the window. I'd trailed her to Lawler's place, and I was outside watching them when the shot came, a couple yards away. It nearly deafened me — that, and Stella's scream. I was dazed; before I could turn around, whoever had been there in the alley with me had already vanished. And Reed Lawler was dead."

"So you don't have any idea who did the shooting? Although he was close enough that you could practically have reached out and touched him?"

Ramsey made a tired gesture. "I know you don't believe me. But I'm telling you the truth."

"If you didn't kill Lawler, why did you run?"

"Why wouldn't I? Why stand there and wait for somebody to come and arrest me for murder? I didn't have any business in that alley; and I'd had plenty cause to do murder. I knew damned well how it would look!"

"Did you?" Gentry looked at him carefully, discerningly. "Did you really figure it all out, Abel — as cooly as that? Or — did you just lose your head, and start running?"

Angry spots of color seeped into the man's bony face. His hands clenched, fell open again. "Damn you —"

"Don't get mad," said the sheriff, shaking his head quietly. "I'm just trying to go past what you want to tell me, to what really happened. And you're right — I do know you pretty well. I hope you'll believe me," he added earnestly, "when I say I'm still your friend, Abel. I don't think you killed him. I hope I can prove it."

He pushed away from the desk, took a step or two across the stuffy room. Whirling back suddenly, he hurled an unexpected question. "Just what were Stella and Lawler talking about?"

Abel Ramsey gave a start. "They — that is, I don't know!"

"You don't?" The sheriff frowned, suspiciously. "You were right outside the window, and the window was open. You mean you couldn't hear *anything,* not even though they were talking in ordinary tones?"

"No. I didn't hear anything."

He was lying, of course. The fact was plain in the look of him, in the way he held onto himself and made his eye meet Gentry's in spite of the desire to break gaze and escape that hard scrutiny. But a stubbornness had settled on Ramsey and the sheriff knew he would not be able to break it down. He had struck a dead wall, here.

He lost his patience and swore a little: "I wish the hell you'd tell me the truth! You hold things back and I can't help you much." Getting no answer, he went to the door and called the jailer in. "Give him a receipt for his belongings," he told the man. "I've got to get back out there in a hurry and see if I can do any good."

"You — you aren't locking me up!" Ramsey had his arm in a convulsive grip.

The sheriff looked at him squarely. "I haven't any choice. There's enough evidence against you to hold you, at least until you're ready to give me a straight story. If I didn't, a lot of people would be thinking I'd let friendship interfere in the plain course of duty — and they'd be right!" He added, "I'll see that you get legal aid, of course. Meanwhile, if you really want to help me find out who killed Lawler, you won't make trouble!"

Minutes later, with the distasteful thing done and Abel Ramsey occupying a cell in the courthouse basement, Tyler Gentry came tramping out upon the steps of the building and paused a moment, filling his lungs with the crisp night air and frowning over the next part of his job. There would be little sleep for him tonight. He'd have to check up with the coroner; take another look — by lantern light — at the alley outside Lawler's room; maybe try for another word with Stella Ramsey, if the doctor had her in shape to talk coherently. After that —

His thoughts boggled suddenly, grizzled head jerking sharply at the meaning of what his sense of smell had just brought him. Smoke — acrid, irritating! The sheriff ran a sweeping look over the sleeping street before the courthouse; then turning, he hurried down the steps to search the sky in that direction. At once he saw it, and gasped.

A fan of ruby light hung above the houses of the town, their pointed gables and squared false fronts etched blackly against it. Sparks spewed upward; it seemed to Gentry's shocked brain that he could all but hear the crackling of the distant fire, feel the heat of it.

"It's Great Western!" he breathed, hollowly. "My God! What more can happen in one night?"

Tearing himself loose from that spot, he started running heavily toward the fire; and only now he became aware of men's shouts, and the clamor of a steel triangle putting its warning across the night. This night was certainly one that Dragoon town could talk about for years to come: the dance, that had been broken up by a bloody slugging brawl, would have been event enough, without its being followed by murder and now, within the hour, by a fire that seemed on the point of taking the entire Ramsey establishment, stock and equipment.

When Tyler Gentry, panting hard, came in on the place, the entire yard behind its high board fence was seething with excitement. He could really feel the heat of the flames, now. They outlined the framework of the big stock barn, and the building was going fast. The screaming of trapped horses, the thud of frenzied hoofs striking stall partitions, carried above the fire sound and the yells as men dashed through the gaping double doors and were silhouetted there bringing the maddened animals out to safety.

At one side, freight wagons lined the fence and a couple at one end of the row made separate, flaming torches. More men were struggling with these, fighting to roll them free before more of them caught. Tyler Gentry joined in, throwing his solid weight against one of the big wheels and straining with legs braced to help move the ponderous vehicle out of line.

Flames, roaring in canvas above his head, licked at him with their heat and he ducked his head into the protection of a shoulder.

The wagon rolled forward and he staggered for balance. He ran a sleeve across his sweating face and left a broad streak of black soot to brand his forehead.

Quick work had saved the rest of the wagons and the two stages: Gentry turned next to the stock barn, where the last of the horses were now, apparently, being rescued. Many of them had broken loose and were running wild about the enclosure, neighing their terror at the sight of fire on every side of them. Tyler Gentry swerved as one of the beasts floundered blindly past him, to go plunging into a knot of men yonder and split them apart in an outburst of shouts.

Someone called the sheriff's name and he turned. It was that clerk — that Paul Becker whose cool, citified ways had always faintly irritated him. He was a changed man now, however. Only sketchily clothed, and black with soot, he had got a lungful of smoke and he could hardly talk for the spasms of coughing that doubled him up between words. "It's terrible!" he choked. "Just missed being a total loss. We saved the horses and most of the rolling stock; but the barns — all that feed, and freight, and equipment —"

"How'd the fire happen?" Gentry demanded.

"It didn't!" Becker's smoke-rasped voice was grim. "It was set! Ask Nelson, the watchman. He broke them up and put a bullet into one of them, or they'd have finished this job!" Then, as Gentry would have turned away to hunt out the old man, "Have you seen Ramsey?"

The sheriff flashed him a look. "Why, yes. He's in jail. Hadn't you heard?"

"Jail! What do you — ?"

"Maybe you better go talk to him — say I said to let you in. I ain't got time to answer questions."

The sheriff broke away and left him standing there, staring. Minutes later he located the old watchman, Joe Nelson, and collared him. "I understand you saw this fire started?"

The old man was almost too excited for coherence. "They was three of the skunks, Sheriff! They snuck in across the fence and, me being a bit deef, I never noticed nothing before they had the barn going and was working on the rigs. I had my gun on me and I opened up and drove 'em off. Shot one of 'em too! Got him pretty bad, I figure."

"Did you manage a look at their faces?"

The old man said yes. "Wasn't anybody I knew — just a bunch of toughs, I figure, down from the hills. The one I plugged was a skinny kind of gent, with a short black beard cut off square. When they scattered, making their getaway, he rode off that direction." Nelson pointed a gnarled finger into the darkness beyond the fence, toward the north and west.

"You're sure?" Gentry made his swift decision then. One was hurt, and he had only a few minutes' headway. Reed Lawler's murderer had already escaped and there seemed little chance of picking up that trail now. Better, thought the sheriff, to give himself at each moment to the job in which he stood the best hope of accomplishing something.

He whirled and shouted at the crowd who were watching the freight barn burning. "Come on! I want a posse! We can't do any more here — get mounts and come with me. And let's hurry it up!"

Vern Jackman was only beginning to realize how very badly he was hurt. He felt as though a fire raged in the middle of his body, growing fiercer as the first bullet shock left him. The running of his horse had become suddenly a trip-hammering source of torment, battering him with every stroke of hoof against the earth. When he could take no more he reined in finally, thrust a hand against his belly and felt the warm stickiness.

Sick and giddy, he hunched there in the saddle and mouthed feeble, bitter curses. He swore at the old man whose wild shot had done this to him; he swore at the two cut-throats who'd scattered and left him to manage the best he could by himself. He cursed the man who, panicky at the shortness of time and at the Ramseys' reluctance to give in, had ordered burning the stables as a final, frenzed effort to clinch their ruin.

Still, he would need something more than oaths to help him now. He was getting lightheaded, he thought. It took the hard grip of a hand on the pommel to keep him upright, and the whole expanse of starlit earth seemed to be circling slowly about him, like a vast turntable with himself in the center. The horse, made restive at the smell of blood, stamped and the shifting of the saddle almost sent its rider tumbling.

A terrible thirst was on him. Jackman lifted his hand, shakily, ran the back of it across his mouth. The lips were dry but his face was sweat-beaded, fevered. He thought: Looks like you played out your luck this time, fellow!

With an effort of will he got himself in hand and, knees locked to brace himself in the stirrups, sent the horse forward again. But he knew he wasn't going to make it. He couldn't tie himself in the saddle, and again, even if he reached the hills, he couldn't save himself from bleeding to death. He had to have help. And there was only one place where he had even a slim hope of getting it.

He worked on this thought, as the horse went forward at its own pace across the uneven, rolling bunch grass swells. He wasn't entirely sure of the location of the place he had in mind, but he thought he could find it if his wits didn't give out on him. He had to find it. He squinted painfully at the stars, trying to take his bearings.

After what seemed like endless hours he found himself at the crest of a rise, with the outlines of a ranch headquarters showing below him — buildings, corrals, a round water tank with the gaunt shape of a windmill standing over it. The place was sleeping, without lights. Vern Jackman sat and looked at it for some time, his mind sluggish and almost vacant of thoughts. But some gleam of logic told him: This wouldn't be it. Too big. . . . So, pulling back, he circled the sleeping ranch and kept on. There was little hope left in him now — hardly more than a blind, unreasoning instinct to keep him going. He had set a goal for himself and he went after it with the tenacity of a wounded animal.

He picked up a wagon road through the sage and bunch grass, presently, and started following it principally because the horse liked the easier going and he was himself too far gone to argue. The clop of hoofs on hard-packed ruts echoed through him. And then surprisingly the movement stopped and its cessation caused him to lift his head, stupidly. The mount had halted in front of another house. This one showed a yellow square of window light. It didn't bulk very large against the stars. It might be the place.

Someone was moving inside, coming to the door. Jackman lifted a long leg and with an effort hoisted it across the back of the horse. His boot touched earth; then the expenditure of energy proved too much and he went clear down, to hands and knees. He was hunched over like that when the door opened, running a widening pattern of light across him. A man shaped up there blackly.

Jackman's gun barrel winked light as he pawed it out of leather and brought it up. The lamp was shining directly in his face and he blinked and tried to say something, but his voice was stuck somewhere in his throat.

He heard Dan Temple's exclamation, then, and Temple's quick stride forward. He thought, incredulously: I made it! And then Vern Jackman let himself go. Only Temple's quick reach and grab kept him from sliding forward prone upon his face.

It was no particular job for Temple to get the hurt man lugged inside and stretched out upon the single bunk, because Vern Jackman weighed little. But, that done, Dan hardly knew what to do next. He had some skill with gunshot wounds but this one was beyond him. The bullet had torn a hole through Jackman's lean middle from which the purple blood pumped steadily, and with all he had already lost it hardly looked as though anyone could do much for him. Wash it clean, bind it up, perhaps. But even surgery would not be good for much to him, now.

Still, Temple fetched water and clean cloths and set to work to do what he could. He moved stiffly, still bruised and sore from his encounter with Lawler; and his thoughts were still too full of his own affairs for even this to break deeply into their dark course. One part of his mind continued to go over and over the futile treadmill of defeat and lost hopes, while another portion directed the working of his hands. There was not enough left to give more than the vaguest and briefest thought to what might have happened to Jackman, and how he came to be here.

It was Jackman himself who jarred him out of this mood, with an abrupt question that was startling because Dan didn't know the man had regained consciousness. Jackman said, his voice weak but startlingly clear: "Pretty bad, ain't it?"

Temple looked at him. Jackman's face looked more gaunt than ever, and his pale eyes held a glaze of pain; but the secret smile was on the thin lips, as sharply etched as before. Jackman said, "Got anything to drink? I wouldn't want to die thirsty!"

"Sure." He got a bottle from the shelf, poured into a tin cup and brought it back to the bed. He had to hold Jackman's head while the man drank, in noisy gulps. Then, as the man who had been his friend lay back, gasping from the burn of the whiskey in his throat, Dan asked gruffly, "You going to tell me what happened to you?"

"Why use up my breath," grunted the other, "when you'll be hearing all about it tomorrow?"

"I won't be around tomorrow," said Dan. "I'm leaving!"

"Leaving?" Jackman's face turned blank

with surprise. "You mean it, Dan? Had enough of trying to be something besides a mugg?"

"Let's not go into it!"

"Well, ain't this a note!" The gunman shook his head a little, on the blankets. "If I'd only known a couple-three hours ago, maybe I wouldn't be lying here now, like this! We'd have made a great team, Danny. I'd have thrown over this job, in half a minute, to have you ride with me."

Dan Temple said, with a trace of bitterness, "You can thank yourself that I've quit! You've done a good job. You've made a complete fool of me, and ruined the people I worked for. You've fixed me so I can't hold my head up in this country any longer. That's the only reason I'm getting out!"

"Sorry, Danny." Vern Jackman's sweat-beaded face looked as though he really meant it. "Sorry you got burned. But you're gonna be better off for it; you wasn't cut out for this kind of thing." He indicated, with a jerk of his head, the crude interior of the shack, and all the heartbreak and toil that it symbolized. He added, "Once I'd got started on this job it wasn't easy to quit — not even for you, Danny. Especially, at the kind of money he was payin' me."

"He? You mean Lawler?"

Jackman made a face. "Not that ape! He was only takin' orders, himself. It takes plenty of backing to call yourself your own boss, Danny. You've tried it and you found out, I guess. But the guy that hired me to break the Ramseys —" He shook his head. "Don't ask me to name names, fellow. I got a little more loyalty than that."

"You don't have to name him," said Dan Temple, suddenly, and a new and peculiar expression had built itself upon his face. "It just occurs to me that I can probably guess!"

Vern Jackman's colorless eyes probed his. "Beginning to use that brain, finally?" And then the secret smile twisted out of shape as a spasm of pain broke it apart. "Oh, God!" groaned Jackman, in savage agony.

Dan was moving toward him when the sudden rattle of a racing horse, hard-ridden, pulled him about to face the door. Reining in before the shack, the rider was calling his name in a frightened voice — the voice of Ruth Chess; and wonderment and alarm sent him quickly to lift the bar and throw the door open. She was there, staring wildly at him. "Ruth!" he cried. "What's wrong?"

She flung an arm toward the night. "Hurry, Dan! They're coming! Gentry and his men — I think I only beat them out by a minute or two. Don't you understand

222

what I'm saying?" she persisted, as he only stared at her. "You've got to ride!"

Chapter Eleven

Utter incomprehension held Dan Temple. Only one thing in the words she said made sense — the fact that she apparently thought him to be in some danger, and that she had cared sufficiently to want to bring him warning. This was hard to believe, but greater still was the effort to understand what could have put such terror in her.

He put a hand on her arm. "Please!" he exclaimed. "Quiet down, Ruth, and tell me what it is you're trying to say! Why should the sheriff be coming here? If it's anything to do with that trouble I had with Lawler tonight —"

She made a gesture of despair, "*I* don't know what it is you've done. We left for home right after — right after the trouble at the hall. And just a few minutes ago, I was wakened by the sound of a lot of riders in the yard, and the sheriff was with them, talking to Dad. Your name was mentioned, but that was all I could make out. So I got dressed in a hurry and started for here, while they were still talking, to warn you. They're coming, along the wagon road — I only made a few miles on them by taking every short cut I knew. You've only got a matter of minutes."

Dan's face hardened suddenly. "I understand. You think I'm guilty of something. You see a sheriff's posse headed my way and you take it for granted I've done something wrong even though you haven't heard anybody say so! Is that your opinion of me?"

"Oh, I — I don't know what I thought!" she cried. "Only — *Listen!*" Dan Temple heard it, too — the growing rumble of several horses, drawing instantly nearer. Then the girl's hand seized his and she was talking fast, pleading with him.

"There's still a moment! I saw your bronc, in front of the house — still saddled, and badly lathered. Mine's fresher. Take him, Dan! I'll take yours, and let the posse have a glimpse of me and draw them off — they'll never guess the trick, by starlight. Before they do, you'll have had your chance to make a start for the hills. . . ."

"But, girl!" he exclaimed, staring at her. "Do you realize what you're offering? Don't you know you'd be risking your neck?"

She faced him directly. "There isn't time to argue, Dan. Of course I know!"

"And for me — you'd do that? Even assuming the sheriff had reason to be hunting

224

me?" Dan Temple could only stand like that, motionless, and take the measure of her offered sacrifice. He shook his head, dumbly. "Why, Ruth?"

It was as though he had never really seen her before. She was suddenly beautiful — her cheeks flushed, her brown hair uncombed and wind-tangled, her eyes glistening with unshed tears. "Oh, Dan — Dan!"

The sound of his name, the way she said it, told him all she had to reveal. And it showed him, also, the full extent of his own blindness. "I didn't know!" he exclaimed. "I never guessed you felt this way —"

But now the drum of approaching hoofs was very near, drawing in unmistakably toward the homestead shack. And Ruth Chess moaned, "You've waited too long. It's too late! Oh, Dan Temple, why wouldn't you — ?"

Her answer came from an unexpected source. Until that moment, distraught as she was, she hadn't noticed the man in Dan Temple's bunk. Now as Vern Jackman spoke, she whipped a startled glance in his direction; the outlaw was seated on the edge of the bunk, clinging to it with both hands, and his glassy eyes had a kind of desperate wildness in them. He said, "Danny wouldn't leave, for the best reason in the world: it ain't him they're after! You see, you made a kind of a natural mistake. It happens that bronc out front belongs to me — and *I'm* the gent they been chasing clear from town!"

Ruth lifted a blank and uncomprehending look from the outlaw's tight face to Dan's. The latter, realizing he had almost forgotten Vern Jackman in this moment of drama, left her and hurried to the bunk. "Quick!" he ordered. "If you think you can get on your feet, let me help you into that corner behind the curtain. I'll stall them off someway."

The tucked-in smile that quirked the outlaw's thin-lipped mouth widened; but the only expression in his face was that of the pain that gripped him. He said huskily, "Sure, Danny — I can get on my feet. But I'm not hiding behind any curtain."

He came up off the bunk, pushing himself erect; the sweat was gleaming on his hollowed, bearded cheeks and it took all his strength to stay like that, swaying. Dan Temple reached a hand to steady him but he shrugged it off with an angry gesture. "I'll do this my way, Danny!" he growled, his voice rough and throaty.

Head thrust forward, he was scanning the room, searching for something. Then he saw it — the sixgun Temple had taken from him and laid upon the square center table. He lurched forward, shoving past Dan, and picked the weapon up in his long fingers.

The thunder of the arriving horsemen was all around them, now, filling the night with the throb of hoofs and jingle of bit chains.

Vern Jackman threw a last look at the man who had ridden beside him, on other trails, in another day. "So long," he said. "So long, Danny!"

"Wait — !"

Dan Temple, only then understanding, made a move forward; but he moved too slowly. Because Vern Jackman had already reached the door, and shoving past the astonished girl, he went through it on uncertain stumbling legs. He struck the jamb with the point of a gaunt shoulder and it unsteadied him, caused him to reel drunkenly as he went out into the yard. He was still trying to get his balance when the men of the posse saw him and knew him for the one they were after.

Dan, himself striding toward the door, heard the shouts, and the first report of a gun. Vern Jackman had fired that shot. He had taken a tentative step toward his ground-reined horse and then, knowing he would never reach it, had swung back to face the posse with gaunt shape bent forward on braced legs, and the revolver leaping in his hand. Straight into the milling crowd of horsemen he threw his fire, raising a startled chorus of yells that mingled with the report of the gun. Horses pitched and squealed.

What followed was inevitable. It was vain for Tyler Gentry to shout: "Hold it! We want him alive!" Too many excitable men had weapons in their hands, and the sheriff's voice was lost in the sudden roar of half a dozen guns. At the close distance, even Jackman's bony figure was a target too plain to be missed. He took their bullets. He jerked half-around, under the force of them. And after that he dropped, and dust and acrid, swirling powder smoke eddied above his prone, sprawled shape.

For a moment, an awed silence dropped over the mounted men in the aftermath of sudden death. Slowly they got their horses quieted. Then with an angry curse the sheriff was swinging down and moving forward, and some of the others began to leave their saddles and crowd after him.

Dan Temple, in the doorway of the shack, turned and spoke quickly to the girl: "You stay in here and keep out of sight! It won't do any good for them to know you're here!" And he too moved toward the knot of men that had clustered about Jackman's body.

Sheriff Gentry had not recovered from his first fury at the posse members. "Damned, itchy-fingered rummies!" he thundered, withering glare sweeping the abashed faces about him. "What good does he do us this way? I wanted to make him do some talking, but you never gave me a chance. I —" He subsided with an angry shake of his head, realizing the futility of such talk. Scolding these men wouldn't bring the prisoner to life again.

Then Dan Temple said, from the edge of the circle: "He was bad hurt — dying on his feet. You wouldn't have got anything out of him, anyway."

Quickly interest shifted to him. The light from the door lay across the faces of these men as they turned. Tyler Gentry said, in his heavy voice, "What have you got to tell us about this, Temple?"

For just an instant, Dan hesitated. He would have to lie, and he didn't want to. But Vern Jackman had made this sacrifice for him and he had to say what Jackman would have wanted, and not waste the life that his old friend had given for him.

He said, "I can't tell you anything. Whoever he is, he came and routed me out of bed and made me bandage the bullet hole in him. He had a gun on me; and besides, a

229

man as badly hurt as he was —" Dan shrugged. "Naturally, I did what I could. Then we heard the horses."

Gentry considered this. "We trailed him from town," he said, "as far as the Chess place. Mark had seen nothing of him but thought he might have headed this way. . . . You're sure you never saw him before?"

"Never," lied Dan. He added flatly, "Are you trying to tie me in with something, Gentry? If so, I wish you'd talk plain!"

He faced the sheriff and a note of danger hung in the air between them. Members of the posse, looking on, unconsciously held drawn breaths as they sensed something building here.

Then the sheriff said, slowly, weighing his words: "I don't just know what I think about you, Temple! There's been some damn peculiar things. Like that day we rode to Antelope, on the stage, and found the freight wagon burning — remember? I followed you, that time; I know where you went from there, but I never been able to figure out why. I jailed you once because I didn't trust you, and I've been tempted a time or two since. But —" He shrugged. "Well, maybe it's a kind of a hunch I've had, that we're really on the same side in this business. Anyhow, I'm not making any charges against you, Temple — and some-how I don't expect to be!"

"That's damned generous," grunted Dan Temple, shortly. He knew the sheriff had, in effect, made an overture toward truce between them, but he was not in a mood for it — not just then.

Gentry turned away. "Well, let's get this gent's body onto a horse and be headed back," he ordered gruffly. "Nothing more we can do." And as the group broke up and made for their waiting mounts, Dan Temple asked a final question:

"Maybe you'll be good enough to tell me what it's all about? What did the guy do, to send you after him?"

Gentry heaved himself into saddle before he answered. "Why all he did," the sheriff said, the reins in his hands, "was set fire to the Ramseys' freight yard!"

The news struck like a blow, and it left Dan standing there in the yard, amid swirl-ing dust, for long seconds after the body of horsemen spurred away and left him alone, taking Jackman's body jackknifed and tied across the saddle of his own horse.

It was but slowly that he woke to the fact that not all the riders had gone. One waited, yonder, standing beside his horse and slap-ping rein ends into the palm of one hard hand. As Temple turned to look at this man, he heard him speak with the voice of Tom McNeil — a voice husky with savage anger. "All right, fellow! Where is she?"

When Temple did not answer, the old cowpuncher jerked his rein ends toward the pinto that stood saddled at the corner of the shack. "I know Ruth's pony when I see it, I reckon. Better send her out here or I might be just crazy enough as to try and kill you, Temple!"

Dan turned and called, briefly: "Ruth!" At once the girl appeared in the doorway. At sight of the old man, she uttered his name and went out to him.

"I thought you were at the ranch, Tom!"

"I come on with the posse, of course," he answered stiffly. "I never thought I'd find you, alone with this — this —" He bristled with hatred, staring at Dan across the girl's head, helpless for eloquent speech.

"Ruth came to warn me about the posse!" Dan snapped cutting in on him. "That's the whole reason for her being here."

"Of course it was," exclaimed the girl indignantly. "You ought to know you can trust me, Tom!"

The old puncher looked at her, his seamed face heavy with frowning thoughts. He said, finally, "Sure, girl, I know I trust you, all

232

right. Don't be mad at me, for thinkin' that — well, for thinkin'!" He lifted his hostile stare at Dan again. "This is the gent I don't trust! Incidentally, fellow, how long you been home?"

His sudden question puzzled Dan. "You were at the dance when Reed Lawler and I broke it up. You know what time that was."

"You left town right after the fight? You can prove that, maybe?"

"Just what are you getting at, anyway?"

His face expressionless in the light from the door, Tom McNeil said, "You hadn't heard, maybe, about Lawler being murdered?"

The stunned look Dan Temple gave him was answer enough. "Yeah," Tom McNeil went on, "according to what the sheriff told us there's been more'n enough excitement in town for one night. The burning of the Ramsey yards just sort of capped the climax. But I'm kind of surprised he didn't ask you about that Lawler business, the shot through the window coming so soon after your run-in with the guy."

"If I wanted to kill a man," said Dan coldly, "I wouldn't wait to do it through a window! I took everything I wanted out of Reed Lawler with my fists, and what happened to him after that made no least difference to me."

Old Tom seemed to consider this. He said then, grudgingly, "Yeah, I guess that's how the sheriff would have figured it — and why he never questioned you. Anyway, he's already got Abel Ramsey in a cell. He must figure there's no question about the killing."

"Ramsey!" cried Dan. Things were coming too fast for him; this night was too full of shocks for a brain still fatigued with sleeplessness, and the lingering aftereffects of his battle with big Lawler. He lifted a hand, ran it through tangled hair. He said abruptly, "I'm going back into town! I've got to find out just what this is all about!"

He turned again to the shack, hurriedly gathered holster and gun, his hat, and also a jacket against the night's chill. Nearly forgotten was the promise he'd made himself that he was through with Dragoon town and its problems. What he had learned tonight nullified that.

He knew now that he was still very much a part of this fast-changing picture, and the dizzying succession of events tonight that seemed to be bringing things to some terrifying climax.

He blew out the lamp, hurried to the corral for his mount. Ready to ride, he found

Tom McNeil and Ruth in saddle and obviously waiting for him; he said, "You'd better be getting home, Ruth. I don't want you having to answer any questions."

Ruth's lips parted on a quick protest, but then she caught old McNeil's look and his quick shake of head. "The man's right," said Tom. "It'll look a lot better. No point in anyone finding out where you were tonight — you know how some people make big talk out of nothing!"

"Please!" Dan reined close to her, speaking insistently, earnestly. "And you might give a little thought to what Tom just said — I mean, about the talking people do without any ground for it. Maybe you see, now, you can't always judge by appearances, or the rumors you hear." He squeezed her arm, briefly; took his hand away. "Goodnight, Ruth. And a thousand thanks for what you did tonight."

He pulled away, not asking for any answer. He heard Tom McNeil tell the girl, "You get along, now. I'm heading in to get in on the excitement, and I'll bring you all the news. . . ."

Minutes later, the two men had their horses pointed through the darkness toward Dragoon, their stirrup leathers brushing occasionally but few words passing between them. Dan Temple set the pace and he kept it a stiff one, for concern was high in him over the startling things McNeil and the sheriff had told him.

They caught sight of the slower-moving posse ahead of them presently, and then saw that the latter had reined back to wait for the pair of them to catch up. "Well?" came the sheriff's sharp challenge.

"Figured we'd trail along into town," said Dan.

He sensed the sheriff's eyes studying him closely in the starlight. "Yeah," said Gentry, grudgingly. "You might be of some help, if you could just get them Ramseys to talk to you. I can't drag much out of them, but they might open for you."

"I'll do anything I can," said Temple, and meant it.

So the truce was drawn between these two, and as they headed on across the bunch grass swells the sheriff talked briefly, giving Dan's astonished ears the full account of what had happened in town. "I don't suppose," he ventured, "you got any suggestions to offer as to what the girl was doing at Lawler's place when he was shot?"

Dan Temple could only shake his head. "I certainly don't. I went to the Ramsey house, after the fight, and tried to talk to her; but I couldn't get her to open the door to me. She must have waited until I'd gone, and then started for Lawler's with the gun —"

"I can only figure," said Gentry reluctantly, "that she went there to kill him, herself. She was always strongheaded. No telling what she might have done if she was provoked."

"But you're certain she didn't do it?" Dan insisted.

"Not with that gun. It wasn't fired. Abel says the shot came from the alley, at an angle from the spot where he was standing looking in the window; but he's not telling all the truth. He insists he didn't hear anything of what was going on in the room, but there I've got a hunch he was lying. The window was open, and it isn't likely they kept their voices down. . . ."

It was late enough when they picked up the lights of Dragoon, shining against the darkness; possibly three o'clock, Dan Temple judged, with the outdoorsman's sure instinct for telling time by the feel of the air, by the pattern of the wheeling stars. But excitement held the town tonight. There were an unusual number of lights showing, and the clatter of the returning posse brought men hurrying into the street in search of news.

Tyler Gentry was curt with his answers. He dismissed his riders with thanks for their help, and sent one of them to find the undertaker and have the disposal of Vern Jackman's body attended to. Afterwards, leaving their mounts to stand before the courthouse, he and Temple went up the broad steps and into the jail office.

They met Judge Homer just emerging from the cellblock; the jurist's face held a look of disdain as he pulled a chaw off his pocket tobacco and wiped the back of a hand across his brown-stained mouth. "Been talkin' to your prisoner, Sheriff," he said shortly. "Wouldn't represent him on a bet. Any fool could see he murdered the man. Was I trying his case, I'd hurl the book at him!"

Gentry gave him a dry look. "You don't waste any time getting to a verdict, do you?" he grunted. "I'm sure as hell glad I never came up before you, in the days when you was on the bench!"

He shoved past the old man and Dan trailed him down the iron-treaded steps, into the bleak, damp corridor. Remembering the night he had spent here, Dan Temple already began to feel the miserable chill of the place creep into him. All but one of the cells was empty. Abel Ramsey, a crumpled

238

and dejected figure of a man, looked up from where he sat on the iron bunk with shoulders bent forward, forearms across his knees. His face was haggard, seemingly more hollowed-out than it normally appeared; his eyes were red-rimmed, his face bruised by the mark of a fist.

Tyler Gentry turned a key in the lock, swung the cell door open. He said, "Here's somebody would like to talk to you a minute."

Not rising, Abel Ramsey stared as though in disbelief as Dan walked into the cell. He said, "What do you want?"

"To help you," said Dan. "If I can — and if you'll let me. How about it?"

Sardonic humor pulled at Ramsey's bloodless mouth. "You really think there's anything anybody could do, now? After what's happened tonight — the yards burned out — me sitting here — ?"

"There's plenty we can do," said Dan calmly. He lowered himself onto the bunk beside the prisoner, held out his bag of tobacco and book of papers; when Ramsey didn't even look at them, he proceeded to build a smoke for himself, talking around the string of the bag dangling from between his teeth, as his eyes watched the work of his quick, sure fingers.

"First," he said, "we can find out who murdered Reed Lawler, so we can set you loose from this jail. But in order to do that it would help a lot if you'd decide to tell everything you know about it — everything you heard through the window tonight, before the shot."

"So you're here to pump me, is that it? Tyler sicked you on me. I thought he was my friend!"

Dan put the tobacco away, and licked and smoothed down the wrapper of the cigarette he'd finished. "He is your friend. As for you and me — why, we've had our differences, but that's no reason why I shouldn't want to help you now. Especially as you're Stella's brother."

"Stella!" The man lifted his head, turning a long and narrowed look on him. "Stella," he repeated. "Are you in love with her?"

Dan took a long time with his answer, his eyes on the matchstick that he held against his thumbnail ready to strike. It was the first time he had faced that question squarely, and now that the moment came the true answer to it was not as easy to find as he might have thought, once.

He snapped the match; it cracked sharply, and its flame leaped against the gloom of the cell. "I'm not sure," he said slowly; "to be frank with you. A lot of things have happened. But whether I do or not, I still feel a responsibility for her."

"Well, you needn't!" Ramsey's voice was suddenly savage with some suppressed emotion. "Don't waste your time thinking it. You're too good for her, Temple — even a man like you deserves better than that!"

Deliberately, Temple put the match to his smoke, got it burning. He said then, shaking out the light, "That's kind of strong, Abel, since I know what you think of me."

"Listen!" A hand gripped his arm, suddenly — a bony, trembling grip. "Why do you suppose I've been keeping my mouth shut about this business tonight, at Lawler's? Because I was ashamed! Because I don't like anyone, friends or strangers, to know the truth — to know what kind of thing there is in my family.

"But I'll tell you, Dan Temple, because it isn't fair for you not to know. You've had Stella on some kind of pedestal, I think, and you've gone through hell trying to keep her there. I haven't any right keeping back from you what I heard through that window!"

And he told his story, pouring it out — keeping nothing back, now that he had breached the dikes of reserve. Temple, listening, felt a kind of sick revulsion begin its churning inside him. The skin stretched tight across the planes of his cheeks until it became like a hard, strange mask; suddenly he found that his jaws were clamped until the muscles ached when he relaxed them, opening his lips on words that sounded false in his own ears.

Ramsey had finished and a silence was in the damp chill of the cell. Dan Temple said, slowly, "You can't blame her — not if she really felt the way she did. No one can choose who he's going to lose his head over; I've found that out —"

But he knew he was only trying to be fair, to be open-minded, and that the effort was wasted. Because, there were the words Abel had quoted, words that had stabbed to the core because he had to believe them: *Nothing between me and Dan Temple . . . in love with me . . . had to keep him on our side because we needed him . . . I hated it. . . .*

He straightened slowly. The cigarette had been crushed to a useless twist of paper in his tightened fingers and he opened his hand and let it drop to the damp floor. "All right," he said, briskly, forcing a change of subject. "The last part of the story — I want to be sure I got it straight. Lawler told her that he was ready to expose the man who had hired him to break Greast Western. You

242

got the impression he was on the verge of naming that man when the shot came and stopped him?"

Ramsey nodded, his eyes on Temple's face.

"And as loud as they were talking, I guess we can figure whoever shot him must have heard every word as plain as you did, yourself. It's more than likely he killed Lawler, just at that moment, in order to stop his tongue."

"I see what you mean."

"But you didn't get a look at the killer? How about Stella — do you suppose she might have glimpsed him, through the window?"

"I — don't know. She was facing it, and some of the light might have touched him. I didn't think to look, myself. All I wanted was to get away from there. After what I'd heard I'm afraid I didn't care much what happened to Stella. I simply lost my head, and cleared out —"

Dan Temple rose from the edge of the bunk. "I guess," he said, disliking the thought, "the only thing left is to talk to her and find out what she can tell us. The trouble is," he added, "I have an idea I already know who killed Lawler, and ordered the burning of the freight yard, and all the rest of it. But of course with no more than a guess to work from, there'll be no chance to prove anything."

Before the startled Ramsey could form a question Dan walked out of the cell. Tyler Gentry leaned against the bars and his expression was interesting as Temple came out. Dan said, "You heard it all?"

"Yeah. Including that last remark of yours. Just what did you mean by that, Temple? Who is it you've got your eye on?"

Dan shook his head. "I'm afraid I was thinking out loud. I said it was only a hunch, and probably not a good one. Because you've got all the facts that I have, and if you don't add them the same way then there must be something wrong with my arithmetic. After all, you savvy more about this kind of thing than I do!"

The sheriff saw he was not going to answer his question, and he made an angry gesture. "Well, at least you got Abel to talk — which is something I couldn't do. I think I better turn you loose on the girl."

"Please!" Dan shook his head. "I'd rather not. I — I couldn't talk to her now."

Gentry considered. "I see," he agreed curtly, and turned to lock Ramsey's cell. As he removed the key he told the man inside, "I better leave you here a little longer, Abel. Maybe I can get you out in a few hours, since you did tell us what you knew. I'll do the best I can."

The prisoner, still staring at the floor, didn't lift his eyes. Tyler Gentry turned away, with a jerk of his head at Dan. "Come along."

CHAPTER TWELVE

When they climbed the iron-tread steps and entered the jail office, they found a visitor awaiting them there, with the turnkey; John Evans bounced up from the edge of a chair and the sheriff told him, with small patience, "This is kind of an odd hour, ain't it? What can I do for you?"

"I'm worried, Mr. Gentry," the syndicate man said. He showed it. His cravat was missing and his waistcoat was unbuttoned, only a gold-plated watch chain holding it together across his pudgy middle. "All the things that are going on, I — well, I got to thinking about the freight I have stacked in Lawler's warehouse. He was his own watchman, you know, and now that he's — now that there's no one to keep an eye on the building, anything might happen. I think you should put a guard on it."

"I left a deputy in Lawler's room," said Gentry. "If he's still around nothing's apt to happen."

"But he isn't! He left right after the coroner took Lawler's body away and the crowd scattered. The building is deserted. Any thief could get into it — or for that matter, even the fireburg that burned out the Ramseys. And there's a small fortune in those crates consigned to the Yellow Jack. It would be horrible if anything happened. The company —"

"All right, all right," grumbled the sheriff. "I see what you mean. I'll send a couple of men over there right away." The look he gave Dan Temple was eloquent with tired disgust. He turned to the jailer. "Take care of it, will you? I've got to be getting to the Ramsey place. If the doc doesn't have Stella under a sedative I'm going to make her talk before this night is an hour older — and I'm gonna have the truth out of her!"

"I don't think you are," said Paul Becker from the office doorway. "She's not at the house, Sheriff. She's gone!"

"What!"

Gentry whipped around. The Ramseys' clerk made a strange figure, his hands and clothing blackened by the soot of the freight yard fire, his usually clean-shaven features darkened with a stubble of beard-shadow. He said, "I've just been to the stage office, and found a note from her on my desk. And down at the freight yard they tell me she was there not twenty minutes ago and ordered a team hitched to the stage. Sim Pearson drove for her. They're headed east — toward the railroad!"

A curse exploded from the lawman. "Why, damn her — ! You say she left a note?"

"Yes." Becker's sullen glance cut to Dan Temple. "It's addressed to him."

He held out an envelope and, dazed, Dan crossed to him and took it. The words, "For Dan Temple," were hastily penciled upon the front of it. The flap was unsealed; he took out a fold of paper and thumbed it open, and saw the message in Stella Ramsey's firm, round writing that was thrown out of shape a little by mental anguish and the haste with which it had been inscribed. He read it twice, silently, in growing astonishment:

Dan:
It's horrible and I can't stand any more of it. I'd go mad if I tried to stay and face it longer.
I'll wait for you at the railroad, Dan. Please come to me there. You must! You don't belong in Dragoon — in that sort of life — any more than I did. Don't

worry about the money. I still have a little something and we'll get more. We always can. So don't disappoint me, because I'll be waiting.

With all my love,

Had he not known the writing, he could not have credited the signature at the foot of the page. He looked up from the letter, feeling a slow crawl of sickness within him at the full force of what it had — finally and irrevocably — revealed to him.

So this, he told himself, was Stella Ramsey!

And what of Reed Lawler, who had died in her arms with her kisses on his mouth? What of her brother, who might even now face a charge of murder for all she knew — or cared? Both had been forgotten, apparently, in selfish concern for her own safety, her own future. Still, she wanted Dan Temple, because she thought there would be a place for him in that future. She would use him, and likely she would throw him aside if he lost his usefulness. There seemed no doubt in her mind at all that he would come. . . .

Sheriff Gentry's voice broke in upon the buzzing of his own thoughts, jerked him back to the immediate present. "Well, man!

What does she say?"

He looked about him, at the crowded office whose windows already showed the first faint paling of dawn; at the door where other men waited, listening, in the corridor beyond. Somewhere in the back of his mind a thought was teasing at him, slowly taking shape. He considered it, studying it from every angle, as he held back a moment from answering the sheriffs impatient question.

He looked at Becker. "Have you read this?"

"No!"

The clerk had replied too quickly, too vehemently, and Dan knew he was lying. This gave him a second's pause, because it might spell the failure of his plan. But then he decided, firmly, to go ahead with it.

"Here's what she wrote," he told the sheriff, and pretended to read aloud:

" 'It's cowardly to run but I can't help myself. Because, I was looking right at the window when Reed Lawler died, and I saw the face of the murderer. If he guessed, he would kill me, too. Maybe, when I'm safe, I can decide what should be done about it, but right now I only know I don't dare stay in Dragoon another night —' " Deliberately Dan Temple folded the paper and put it into a pocket.

Someone broke the heavy silence. "You goin' after her, Sheriff? You gonna bring her back and make her testify?"

Tyler Gentry turned on the questioner with a look of scorn. "Kill a good bronc, trying to overtake a stage that's got a twenty-minute start? I ain't that crazy!"

"But she knows who killed Lawler! She says so, in the letter!"

"Yes," agreed the sheriff. "She knows — and when she gets over the shock of this thing, she'll return of her own accord. I know she will," Gentry insisted, still dogged in his faith in the Ramsey spirit. "She'll come to her senses; she'll see it's all she can do, for her brother's sake. . . .

"Now, the lot of you clear out of this office!"

Dan was among the first to obey, shoving a path through the excited crowd. The stern command of purpose lay upon him, and the need for hurry. But before he could quite get clear, a hand grabbed his arm and halted him. Turning, he met Paul Becker's angry stare.

"Just what are you trying to do?" gritted the clerk. "Why did you make up all that about —" He broke off, coloring a little. "All right, so I read the letter! But I still don't like this! Are you trying to get *her* murdered, too? When the man who killed Lawler hears of this, he'll figure she's got to be stopped and silenced before the sheriff gets a chance to talk to her!"

"And do you," replied Dan coolly, "know of any other way to flush him out in the open?"

The other's expression altered; his sullen eyes took on a hard contempt. "Oh. So that's it! You're being clever again, are you? You imagine you can use your brain instead of your gun and your fists? You thickheaded gunman! I'd think you would have learned your lesson by now. . . ."

Dan Temple swung away and strode off before he could lose control; but the Easterner's hard, mocking words seemed to follow him. Probably Becker was right. His scheme to unmask Reed Lawler's killer was naively simple and it exposed Stella Ramsey to a risk he had no right to place on her. But the thing was done, and he could only go ahead with it.

The corridor had already emptied. He went out into the gray light of false dawn; he swung beneath the tie-pole, took the rein of his chestnut gelding and lifted himself into the saddle. Paul Becker had delayed him by just enough that it might itself cause the failure of his plan. This thought laid an urgency upon him, and he was chafing beneath it as he moved away from the courthouse and put his horse into the east-west street that, quartering the town, became the stage road pointing toward the railhead sixty miles distant.

Here he let the chestnut out a little. Beyond the last of the town's sleping houses, the road dipped sharply across a gravel-bottomed stream, shadowed and willow-lined. The gelding's hoofs splashed spray from the cold, swift-paced water; then, topping out on the far bank of the shallow cut, Dan heard movement in the brush and dropped a hand by instinct toward the holstered butt of his gun.

"Temple?" someone called hoarsely, and he recognized the voice of Tom McNeil. As he pulled rein sharply, the old puncher kneed his own mount out of the willows. "I thought it would be you," he said above the runneling murmur of the stream, "but I wasn't sure. . . . Your man's already gone."

For a moment Dan stared at the dimly seen, time-warped shape in the big stock saddle. Apparently McNeil, with seasoned native cunning, had guessed the full nature of the trap he had prepared.

Dan said quickly, "How do you know this? Did you see him?"

"Seen his tracks." McNeil gestured toward the stage road beneath their horses' hoofs. "Rider went through here only minutes ago, on the trail of the stage. Pushin' his bronc hard, too. I figure he must be the one you're after."

Temple considered, frowning. "He can't hope to overtake the stage, of course. But on the other hand he won't need to do that, because a bronc doesn't have to stick to the road.

"The stage takes a wide swing to skirt the southern end of Horse Ridge. It wouldn't take any great shakes of a horseman to cut straight east, cross the ridge and come down on the road before the coach could reach there, even with the start it has on him. After all, Sim Pearson won't be pushing the horses too much; he'll be counting on plenty of time to catch the noon train out of King's Station."

The old puncher said, "That all makes sense. Still, it will be close timing at Horse Ridge. If that's what he has in mind — and it looks like his only chance of catching up — he'll have to hump it some making the connection."

"No more than I will in order to head him off!"

"Then go ahead, Dan Temple, and good

253

luck to you!" grunted Tom McNeil. "I'd only hold you back, on this bonerack I strap my saddle to!"

He lifted a gnarled hand, in salute; Dan Temple, with that constant pressure of urgency upon him, was already sending his gelding ahead, out of the willows, and he only threw a brief "Thanks!" across his shoulder as he pounded past the old man. But he had time to reflect that Tom McNeil seemed to have changed his attitude, in the last hours; his old hostility toward Dan had melted. This pleased him, but there was little time to think about it now.

He had the gelding strung out and running strongly, hoofs beating a steady rhythm from the hard sounding-board of the earth. The stage trace unrolled ahead of him, a dim silver ribbon against the shadowed swells of bunch grass and sage. While it pointed straight eastward he held to it, in order to take advantage of its level, well-worn course. The rolling rangeland swept by, touched to a smoky half-light now as dawn began to swell below the horizon directly ahead.

The light strengthened every moment, ran liquidly along the curve of the earth. Peering slit-eyed into the wind that stung the bruised and knuckle-torn skin of his face,

Dan Temple sought a glimpse of the coach, or of that other horseman he knew was already somewhere ahead of him. But both had too wide a lead on him, and the dip and swell of the earth hampered his vision. He had only to keep pushing, keep his own mount at this hard and steady gait, and hope for time.

Minutes ticked past. The light was growing upon the world, the sky in the east turning now the color of polished steel; objects were taking on depth and dimension, and an occasional low-headed juniper stood out plainly against the deceptive dawnlight. Overhead, stars were paling before the approach of a new day. And now, in front, the shape of Horse Ridge began to lift and cut a hard knife-edge across the smear of increasing brightness.

It was spur from the northern hills, that thrust far out into the flatlands. The ground became more rugged now, beginning to break against the upthrust of the ridge, and there the stage road started its wide, sweeping loop in order to horseshoe about its lower end. Dan Temple pulled his mount to the left instead, and as the road swung away lifted the gelding out of it and swung directly toward the ridge itself.

At once, the going became tougher; but

Dan kept pushing and the chestnut was able to maintain its gait for minutes more. The road was lost to him completely by this time; the slope of the ridge, naked save for a thin scattering of brush and juniper, lifted hard before him. The ground underfoot was slanted and broken. Dan could feel his exhausted horse laboring as it tried to keep up the pace despite the steepening terrain, and the treacherous footing in loose rubble dropped from the eroded face of the ridge.

At last he pulled in, and dropped quickly from the saddle. "All right, fellow," grunted Temple. "We'll take it easier for a while." And, slipping an elbow through the looped reins, he struck out on foot, leading the gelding.

It would not have been too difficult a climb to make, except for the pressure of haste. Sliding gravel was the worst hazard; it shifted and scattered underfoot, seeming to melt away beneath him. By the time he had struggled a third of the way up the slope and the pitch became really steep, Dan was bathed in sweat and cursing the tricky stuff. And when he lost his footing completely to go down in a sprawl that carried him back a dozen feet of hard-won ground, he came up coughing on rock dust and knowing he would have to force himself to take it easier.

He still had the gelding's reins. He swiped dirt and sweat from his haggard face, stood braced on boots planted wide apart in the steep gravel surface while he got his wind and rested for precious moments.

"We'll try it again," he told the gelding.

This time, he plotted his route in advance and he took it in less of a hurried scramble, with a result that he actually made better time. He went up at an angle, quartering across the face of the barren ridge; behind him the gelding followed doggedly with bobbing head, daintily picking its footing. And though the loose rock still dragged at him, still seemed from time to time to melt away under his boots and suck him down, Dan Temple made his way slowly over the shifting and uncertain ground — very gradually the knife-edge ridgetop drew nearer.

Finally man and horse pulled themselves onto that narrow spine of impervious lava rock, and the other face of the ridge lay below them with the range, dun and silver in the gleam of approaching daylight, stretching beyond to the east.

Scanning that panorama quickly, Dan Temple saw the stage road where it looped widely and swung again toward the point of the rising sun. He had to squint against a smear of brightness, shading his eyes with a hand, before he saw the coach itself, and the feather of dust trailing as it rolled away along that ribbon of molten light. It was some three miles distant, he judged, and moving at no great speed behind its six-horse team. Sim Pearson was a vaguely imagined figure upon the box; Stella Ramsey, of course, would be inside.

But in his first swift survey Dan caught no glimpse of the horseman he was trailing and for a moment he thought he had made some miscalculation, that his anxious ride had been for nothing. Then, he saw him.

Out of a shield of stubby juniper at the foot of the ridge the dark shape of a racing horse burst suddenly and was speeding away from him, weaving a sharp course through the broken talus and then leveling out and pointing directly toward the road. Dan saw the rider, hunched forward in saddle. The sight brought his sixgun halfway out of leather; but he shoved it back, knowing the distance was too great and the target too uncertain. Instead, he turned at once and was in the saddle, and looking quickly for the best negotiable way down the yonder slope.

He spotted it almost at once — a slanted outcrop of tough igneous rock projecting beyond the weathered ridge face. It made almost a shelf of resisting lava. Dan kneed his reluctant gelding forward and turned it downslope toward the head of this ledge; and as the animal's hoofs struck the rock he gave it the spurs.

They took that chute of outcropping at a dizzy, dangerous run, with shoe-irons clanging out sparks, and every step holding the possibility of a stumble that could snap the necks of both horse and rider. Then the ledge of rock ended and there was the fan of loose gravel footing the slope. Yet Dan held the horse firmly to the same hard pace. They went down into the soft stuff, sliding and gouging on braced hoofs, and the rock dust ballooned high. At the last minute the gelding almost stumbled and a quick jerk on the reins helped lift it out of that; then solid earth was underfoot again and they flashed ahead, in the wake of the other horseman.

He had already reached the road and was even now reining into it, drumming after the dust plume of the stage coach, not yet himself aware of pursuit. Dan estimated the distances and the timing. It would be very close. Apparently that other rider had had even a harder go than he in crossing the ridge, for with all his lead on Dan he had narrowly made it ahead of him. But he still held a margin of seconds and Dan knew those few seconds could determine the outcome.

The hard-packed surface of the road was under his gelding's hoofs, now, and on this footing it managed a spurt of greater speed — but without gaining any on that other rider. For the gelding was tiring fast; it hadn't been fresh, anyway, when this wild chase started. Now a fleck of foam blew back from its gaping jaws, struck his cheek and stung sharply. That other horse was holding the pace, keeping the relative distance between them; and ahead, the slower-moving stage seemed to be growing momentarily larger.

And now, apparently, Sim Pearson became for the first time conscious of the horsemen bearing in upon his rear. His face showed dimly as he twisted about to peer through the dust haze churned up by the coach wheels. He straightened about again and suddenly Dan Temple saw that the driver was actually slowing, hauling on the ribbons. Pearson, not expecting danger, apparently thought there must be an urgent reason for someone trying to overtake him and meant to halt. Temple gritted clenched teeth. No, you fool! he groaned wordlessly.

Don't slow! Keep going —

There was, he knew then, only one way to stop this. Lifting the heavy sixshooter, he sighted past the bobbing ears and flying mane of his own horse, trying to steady his aim on the dark, dust-blurred shape of that other mount ahead. He hated to kill a horse, but he needed the rider alive; moreover, shooting from saddle, he couldn't choose too small a target. So, fighting the jar of his own mount's running stride, he drew a bead; but it was still little more than a snap shot.

The weapon cracked, above the pound of hoofs. Acrid smoke swept back into his face and he blinked against it. The other horse was still running strongly. He was about to fire a second time when with an exclamation he held his hand.

That bullet had found a target, after all. The man in the saddle had suddenly lost the rhythm of his mount's gait; he was reeling badly, jarred by the pounding. And now, even as Dan Temple registered the fact that chance had done what he had wanted to avoid, the other rider was listing sideward and then plummeting bodily from the back of his horse.

He lit rolling, and went over three or four complete turns before his body came to a stop. The horse kept going, in the dust of the coach. But Dan, reigning quickly, was out of saddle and running forward, still carrying the smoking gun.

Breaking through weeds and brush, he came to a halt above John Evans' limp body, sprawled on its back in the dirt with legs and one arm thrown out grotesquely, the other arm bent back beneath him.

The syndicate man was not dead. A seeping of blood from somewhere beneath him showed that he was badly wounded, but his eyes were open and filled with malignant life as they came to a focus on Dan Temple's dust-streaked face. It seemed to Dan, though, that this was not the John Evans he had known — not the rather contemptible, obsequious sort of man to whom he had paid little more than a cold glance in his few dealings with the syndicate manager. He lay there in his own blood and glared at the one who had brought him down, and his twisted face held now exactly the look Dan had once seen on a wounded coyote, maddened by rage and pain as it turned, snarling, on its enemies.

"Damn you, Temple!" he gritted. "How did you — ?"

"It was a trap," Dan told him. "And you walked into it! Stella Ramsey didn't say anything in her note about seeing you through the window. I made that up, for your benefit. I couldn't think of any other way to force your hand."

"But what pointed you to me? I'd covered my tracks. I'm sure Lawler never talked — though he would have if I hadn't killed him to shut his mouth!"

Dan shook his head. "No, he never said anything except that there was big money behind him — and for some reason I never suspected that he meant you, and the syndicate. Fact is, you gave yourself away, even though it took me a hell of a long time to see the connection. You did it, the day you had Vern Jackman waylay the Yellow Jack freight wagon and take the payroll shipment.

"Only four people heard my plan for running that shipment: the Ramseys, and Paul Becker, and — of course — yourself. And one of that group betrayed the secret, or let it slip. My first guess was Becker, but after he convinced me that he wasn't guilty it took me a spell of floundering around in the dark before I hit on the only other answer. Even then, it didn't make sense, because I took you for what you pretended to me. It never occurred to me you had the cunning, or the nerve, to carry through a thing like this program to break the Ramseys!"

John Evans took it all in silence, except for the growing rasp of tortured breath sawing at his throat. His face, pale and beaded with sweat, twisted in a grimace as Dan finished. "So that was it," he grunted. "I went too fast! But I had to — there was so little time to do the job in —"

From over in the road, Sim Pearson yelled across the stillness: "Temple! What the hell is going on?" Unnoticed by Dan, he had halted the coach and turned it to circle back. He called now from the box, "You got a dead man there?"

Dan turned, briefly. He saw Stella Ramsey at the window of the coach, staring, her face colorless and lips parted. He answered Pearson's question: "Not dead, though close to it. But maybe, with the stage, we can get him back to a doctor in time to save him. Come down and give me a hand."

"Sure," grunted the driver, and as he started wrapping the ribbons about the brake handle Dan Temple turned back to the hurt man. "Think you can stand?" he asked.

"You'll have to help me," John Evans gritted painfully. "I think my arm is broken."

Dan had to pouch his smoking gun to do

it; he stepped forward, reaching to take the man and help him to his feet. And that was the moment when Stella Ramsey screamed.

For the arm that was twisted back beneath John Evans' body was not broken; he had said it to maneuver his enemy into an impossible position — hands empty, body off balance as Temple stepped forward. Now, with startling speed, Evans whipped that arm forth and the barrel of the weapon it held streaked reflected light in the early sunrise. Dan glimpsed the blur of movement, and the hatred in the man's face. There was no chance to draw against it, and at that point-blank range a sixgun bullet would tear him in two.

He threw himself violently sideward, groping instinctively for holster as he went down. The gun in Evans' hand blasted; he felt the heat of it against his body, and then the solid jar of the earth striking him. But — by how narrow a margin he was never to know — the bullet missed.

A little shakily, Temple lifted his own gun from leather as he rolled up to his knees, ready for a second shot from Evans. It didn't come. That sudden exertion had been too much; Evans had husbanded his last strength for the chance to catch his enemy off guard, and he had spent it all in making his shot. He lay perfectly motionless, eyes half-closed and with only a rim of white showing beneath the drooping lids. The gun had dropped from the limp hand. The syndicate man lay there with his meticulous clothing disarrayed and fouled by his own blood; and he was plainly dead.

Dan was just coming to his feet when Stella Ramsey reached his side and her hands clutched at him. "Dan! He didn't — you aren't hurt?"

"No," he said, turning to her. "I'm all right."

"Thank God!" She was trembling, visibly shaken. She was dressed in a gray traveling suit that accented the pallor of her cheeks and the bright flame of her auburn curls. She said, "Oh, Dan! I thought he had murdered you. . . . You got my note? And you came after me — you came to take me away from this horrible country! I knew you would! I knew you loved me enough. . . ."

He said, "I'm going to take you back, Stella. Back to Dragoon. It will do you no good, ever, to run away — and there's nothing now to run from." He pointed at the lifeless huddle that was John Evans. "There's your enemy. The Ramseys will have no more trouble, after this. There's rebuilding to be done, and your brother will

266

need help in doing it."

She was a moment in answering. Yonder, Sim Pearson stood beside the coach, staring at them with a puzzled expression. Eastward, the sun was above the horizon now; it laid its long, golden light across the far-stretching plains. Dan Temple looked down at the girl, and saw the flush of sunrise placed upon her flawless skin of cheek and throat, the rich light it kindled in her hair. He felt the nearness of her, the pull of her attractions upon his male nature.

"It's up to you, Dan," said Stella, her voice husky and warm now. "Whatever you say — wherever you want to take me — you know I'll go with you. . . ."

The man in the livery buggy came rolling up the wagon track toward the sod-and-shake cabin, a curious look on him as he surveyed the homestead layout; he didn't seem to know quite how to take what he saw. As he curbed his rented horse before the door, a tall, brown-skinned man in jeans and work boots came around the corner of the shack and, nodding greeting, strolled over to the buggy.

The visitor returned the nod, studying the face of the other — the lean, strong jaw, the nose with the small white tracery of a scar across it, the gray eyes and the hair that was grizzling a little though apparently not with age. He said, "I'm looking for a man named Dan Temple."

"You can stop looking," said the other, and smiled, his eyes mildly curious.

The man in the buggy offered his hand. It was white and soft and carefully manicured, and he winced a little under the other's strong grip. He said, without further preface, "My name is Rogers, Mr. Temple. I represent the Illinois Land and Development Company —"

"What we out here call 'the syndicate'?" Dan Temple interpreted.

"I suppose that's right." The man sobered quickly, frowning over serious thoughts. "I'm here investigating the things that have been going on under our late local manager — John Evans. It's a terrible business — terrible. Needless to say, my company very much regrets having been in any way connected with or responsible for what has happened!"

Dan Temple said, "I guess I can understand that, Mr. Rogers. Won't you step down, and stay a while?"

"Not today," said the syndicate man quickly. "I can see you're a busy man, and I wouldn't want to take up your time. I can say what I came for in a few words — and get your answer."

"My answer?"

"At least, your promise to think it over. This is the proposition, Mr. Temple: the company plans shortly to put a good deal of money into development of its properties in this section, especially its mine holdings back in the Dragoons. We mean to reopen a lot of those old mines, try modern and better methods of working them. When we mentioned this to Evans, a few months ago, we told him we were interested first of all in gaining control of freighting facilities into the Dragoons, to assure ourselves of low supply costs; we asked him to look into the matter and see if it could be done."

Dan Temple smiled bleakly. "I guess I can fill in the rest! Friend Evans was so anxious to please that he promised to get it for you at your own price — but without telling you the methods he would have to use doing it. I suppose it would have meant a bigger job for him, and better pay, if he could just impress you with what a smart operator he was."

"You've got the picture. Naturally, we've been appalled to learn the methods Evans did use; the company is holding itself liable for the damage he worked against the

269

Ramsey people, and we're dealing now for a cash settlement of their claims against us. Also, of course, we'd like to buy them out, at a decent price, if they're of a mind to sell; otherwise, we'll arrange for the handling of our increased freight needs at a figure suitable to both of us. . . . But, I'd suppose you've heard all this before."

"Yes," said Dan. "I've been talking to the Ramseys."

The syndicate man said, "Then I'll get to the point. We still need a man to fill Evans' job — or rather, the job Evans would have been in line for if he hadn't overreached himself. We want a general field manager here, and this time we want a man we know we can trust. We'll pay well for him. . . . What do you say, Temple?"

The other could only stare at him, not comprehending at first. He blurted, then, "You mean me? You're asking me to take it?"

"Why, you've got a high reputation in these parts," said Rogers, smiling. "I notice people hereabouts seem to swear by you, Temple. The sheriff, in particular — and that clerk of the Ramseys', Paul Becker, who's been talking an arm off me about your brains and ability —"

Slowly, Dan Temple lifted a hand and ran

it through his hair.

"You've struck me all of a heap!" he said. "The idea's too sudden for me to give you an answer right away. Frankly, I'm not at all sure I could manage anything that size." He indicated, with the sweep of a hand, the homestead layout. "This is the most I've ever tackled — and I haven't done too good a job of it, so far!"

The syndicate man only smiled. "We're willing to take the risk, if you are. But just think it over, will you? And let me know?"

"Why, sure. I'll go along that far with you. And either way — thanks many times for the offer!"

After they had shaken hands again, and the syndicate man had turned his buggy and started back through spring sunshine across the rolling flats toward town, Dan Temple stood for a long moment staring after him with the same look of numbed bewilderment.

He turned only when the girl came into the door of the cabin, behind him, and spoke his name: "Well, Dan. Are you going to take him up?"

Dan Temple walked over to her slowly. "I — don't rightly know! You think I could handle it? You think I got the brains?"

"I know very well you can do anything

271

you care to try," she told him, with quiet confidence.

He looked about him. "I dunno, though," he observed thoughtfully. "I don't think I'd look so good behind somebody's desk. Maybe this place isn't much, but I've put a lot of work into it. I've always thought of myself as being a rancher, one day. . . ."

"If that's what you want the most," she agreed promptly, "tell the man 'no.' "

He grinned his slow grin. "All right, I will then. But — doesn't the future mean any more to you than that?"

"Why," said Ruth Chess simply, "any future is all right with me, Dan — so long as you're a part of it! Didn't you know?"

He saw her lips curved in quiet happiness, as he bent to kiss them.

ABOUT THE AUTHOR

D(wight) B(ennett) Newton is the author of a number of notable Western novels. Born in Kansas City, Missouri, Newton went on to complete work for a Master's degree in history at the University of Missouri. From the time he first discovered Max Brand in Street and Smith's *Western Story Magazine,* he knew he wanted to be an author of Western fiction. He began contributing Western stories and novelettes to the Red Circle group of Western pulp magazines published by Newsstand in the late 1930s. During the Second World War, Newton served in the US Army Engineers and fell in love with the central Oregon region when stationed there. He would later become a permanent resident of that state and Oregon frequently serves as the locale for many of his finest novels. As a client of the August Lenniger Literary Agency, Newton found that every time he switched publishers he was given a different byline by his agent. This complicated his visibility. Yet in notable novels from *Range Boss* (1949), the first original novel ever published in a modern paperback edition, through his impressive list of titles for the Double D series from Doubleday, *The Oregon Rifles, Crooked River Canyon,* and *Disaster Creek* among them, he produced a very special kind of Western story. What makes it so special is the combination of characters who seem real and about whom a reader comes to care a great deal and Newton's fundamental humanity, his realization early on (perhaps because of his study of history) that little that happened in the West was ever simple but rather made desperately complicated through the conjunction of numerous opposed forces working at cross purposes. Yet, through all of the turmoil on the frontier, a basic human decency did emerge. It was this which made the American frontier experience so profoundly unique and which produced many of the remarkable human beings to be found in the world of Newton's Western fiction.

We hope you have enjoyed this Large Print book. Other Thorndike, Wheeler, Kennebec, and Chivers Press Large Print books are available at your library or directly from the publishers.

For information about current and upcoming titles, please call or write, without obligation, to:

Publisher
Thorndike Press
295 Kennedy Memorial Drive
Waterville, ME 04901
Tel. (800) 223-1244

or visit our Web site at:

http://gale.cengage.com/thorndike

OR

Chivers Large Print
published by BBC Audiobooks Ltd
St James House, The Square
Lower Bristol Road
Bath BA2 3SB
England
Tel. +44(0) 800 136919
email: bbcaudiobooks@bbc.co.uk
www.bbcaudiobooks.co.uk

All our Large Print titles are designed for easy reading, and all our books are made to last.